DOCTOR WHO AND THE
INVISIBLE ENEMY

DOCTOR WHO AND THE INVISIBLE ENEMY

Based on the BBC television serial *The Invisible Enemy*
by Bob Baker and Dave Martin by arrangement with
the British Broadcasting Corporation

TERRANCE DICKS

Number 36
in the
Doctor Who Library

A TARGET BOOK

published by
the Paperback Division of
W. H. ALLEN & Co. Ltd

A Target Book
Published in 1979
by the Paperback Division of
W.H. Allen & Co. Ltd
A Howard & Wyndham Company
44 Hill Street, London W1X 8LB

Reprinted 1982 (twice)
Reprinted 1984

Novelisation copyright © 1979 by Terrance Dicks
Original script copyright © 1977 by Bob Baker
and Dave Martin
'Doctor Who' series copyright © 1977, 1979 by the
British Broadcasting Corporation

Printed in Great Britain by
Hunt Barnard Printing Ltd, Aylesbury, Bucks.

ISBN 0 426 20054 3

Contents

1	Contact	7
2	The Host	16
3	Death Sentence	25
4	Foundation	34
5	Counter-attack	45
6	The Clones	55
7	Mind Hunt	65
8	Interface	75
9	Nucleus	82
10	The Antidote	89
11	The Hive	97
12	Inferno	106

I

Contact

Something was waiting out in space.

It drifted between the stars, formless, shapeless, a hazy, drifting cloud, waiting patiently, as it had waited for millennia. It was helpless since it lacked physical form, yet potentially it was all-powerful. Apparently inert, it was filled with life and a fierce, driving purpose. It was waiting for a host.

The space shuttle nosed its way through the asteroid belt, altering course to avoid the larger ones, deflecting the smaller with its energy shields. Inside the little control cabin, the bored three-man crew waited for the long voyage to end.

Meeker was at the controls, staring moodily at the instrument panels. Behind him the captain, Safran, and Silvey, the other crew member, lay on their acceleration couches. Safran was dozing, his worn features relaxed in sleep. Silvey, young and fresh-faced, was awake and restless.

Technically, Meeker was on duty, though in reality he had nothing to do. A steady, self-satisfied instrument-beep announced that the ship's computer was really in charge. It had brought the ship from Earth, soon it would land it safely on Titan, one of the ten moons that circled the giant planet Saturn, 1,430 million kilometres from Earth's sun. This was the paradox of space travel. You selected the brightest, the most determined from thousands of candidates and trained them to a peak of mental and physical skill. Then you surrounded them with computer technology so that only in some million-to-one emergency would their skills ever be needed.

The space radar screen was filled with the blips that marked the track of the asteroids. A particularly large one appeared; the ship tilted in an emergency course-correction.

Meeker decided to stage his own little rebellion. His hands moved over the controls. Silvey looked up. 'What are you doing?'

'Going over to manual.'

'What for?'

'Why not? If I'm going to be banged around, I'd sooner do it myself!' Meeker flicked on the forward scanner and began steering a course through the asteroids, throwing the little ship about in his enthusiasm.

Silvey yawned. 'It's still telling you what to do ...'

'Yes, but at least I'm doing it!'

A sudden lurch nearly sent Silvey from his acceleration couch. 'Oh, come on, Meeker ...'

A second, and even more violent lurch produced a steady, reproachful beep from the watchful computer. Captain Safran opened one eye. 'You're off course, Meeker.'

Meeker wrestled with the controls. 'Sorry, Skipper.'

'Put it back on automatic, Meeker—please.'

Still struggling to complete his course correction,

Meeker muttered, 'I can't ...' He felt a sudden flare of panic as the computer failed to respond. It was as if something had distracted its attention.

Safran got to his feet, leaned over the console and stabbed rapidly at the controls. The alarm signal ceased, there was a musical beep, and the controls locked back on to automatic.

Safran said, 'Titan shuttle captain to computer.'

A musical tone acknowledged his self-identification. 'New course for Titan, please.'

A beep of assent. Lights flashed on the keyboard, and the shuttle adjusted its course.

Safran put a hand on Meeker's shoulder. 'All right, Meeker, that's enough. You're off watch. At once, please.'

Meeker took Safran's place on the couch, while Safran slid easily into the command chair. Automatically he began checking his instruments.

The shuttle was almost through the asteroid belt by now, and the drifting cloud was waiting. As the shuttle approached, the cloud flickered with energy, as if it sensed the presence of approaching life. It thickened, condensed, and began moving purposefully towards the shuttle.

Safran said reproachfully, 'You've lost us three minutes, Meeker!'

'So? Going to be there six months, aren't we?'

'That's not the point!'

'Sorry, Skipper. The thought of six months on Titan ...'

'What's wrong with it?' asked Silvey cheerfully. 'Routine duties, easy life ...'

Meeker nearly exploded. 'I qualified for exploration eight years ago, and what am I? Glorified garage attendant on a planetary filling station!'

Silvey grinned sympathetically. Actually there was some point to Meeker's complaint. But Space Service rules were strict. Everyone had to accept his share of the routine duties, as well as the more exciting and glamorous assignments.

'Your turn'll come,' said Safran consolingly. 'And you'll be glad enough of refuelling bases then.'

Meeker refused to be consoled. 'All I'm saying is why take a real space pilot and——'

An alarm-beep from the computer interrupted him.

'Unidentified organism approaching,' said the computer. 'Changing course to avoid.'

The shuttle veered away from the approaching space cloud. But as it brushed the edge, something within the nebulous mass flared into life, and sent out a fiery tentacle. Lightning flickered around the shuttle for a moment, then died away.

The shuttle moved on, and the cloud began drifting away through space ...

Safran stared at the empty radar screen. 'What was all that about? There's nothing there ... Titan shuttle captain. Report please.'

In a slurred, dragging voice the computer said, *'Contact has been made ...'*

Safran looked at his two crew members. 'Contact?' he said wonderingly. 'What does that mean?'

No one answered him.

Meanwhile another craft was on its way to the same remote edge of the solar system, travelling through the vortex, that mysterious region where space and time are one. It was called the TARDIS and the outside of it resembled an old blue police-box. The inside was a very different matter. The TARDIS was dimensionally transcendental—bigger on the inside than the outside. How much bigger was difficult to say, but an astonishing number of rooms were tucked away inside.

A very tall man with a mop of curly hair marched into one of the control rooms and stood gazing around with an expression of mild displeasure. He was dressed with a kind of casual Bohemian elegance in a long, loose jacket, gaily checked waistcoat and tweed trousers. The outfit was topped with a broad-brimmed soft hat, and an incredibly long multi-coloured scarf dangled round his neck.

The girl who followed him into the control room wore a brief outfit made from animal skins. She moved with panther-like grace and her hand was never far from the knife in her belt. Leela had been brought up as a fighting warrior in a tribe that had regressed from technological civilisation to primitive savagery. She had been the Doctor's companion for some time, and she should have been used to scientific marvels by now—but the TARDIS could still surprise her.

Leela gazed wonderingly around the control room.

It seemed very like the TARDIS control room she was used to, the same many-sided console in the centre But there was one major difference. This control room was all in gleaming white.

Leela looked at the Doctor. 'We've never been here before.'

'*You've* never been here before,' said the Doctor moodily. He crossed to the console, removed a side-panel and began checking something inside.

'Where are we?' asked Leela curiously.

'Number two control room. It's been closed for re-decoration.' The Doctor glared at the console. 'I don't like the colour,' he said accusingly.

'White isn't a colour,' objected Leela.

The Doctor said, 'That's the trouble with computers, always thinking in black and white. No aqua-marines, no blues. No imagination!'

Leela gathered that the TARDIS had the power to redecorate itself on its own initiative. She was about to ask the Doctor why he didn't just order the re-decoration to be changed, when the control room gave a sudden lurch. 'Have we stopped?'

'No, we haven't stopped.'

'Have we materialised?'

'Yes.' The Doctor flicked on the scanner. Some-where in the distance a huge planet hung in space. It was surrounded by a shining ring, a kind of halo.

Leela looked at the screen. 'Where are we, Doctor?'

The Doctor studied instrument-readings. 'The edge of Earth's solar system, somewhere near Saturn ... about 5,000 AD.' He looked at Leela. '5,000 AD, Leela! We're in the time of your ancestors.'

'Ancestors?' Leela's tribe, the Sevateem, were the

descendants of a planetary survey team who had been stranded on a hostile planet.

'That's right. That was the time of the great break-out!'

'The great what?'

The Doctor stared abstractedly at the ringed planet on the scanner. 'The time when your forefathers went leapfrogging across the solar system on their way to the stars. The asteroid belt's probably teeming with them by now. Frontiersmen, pioneers, waiting to spread across the galaxy like a tidal wave—or a disease ...'

'Why a disease—I thought you liked humanity?'

'I do, I do,' protested the Doctor. 'Some of my best friends are human. But when they get together in great numbers, other life-forms sometimes suffer ...'

Saturn is a giant of a planet, an immense globe of gas seven hundred and fifty times the volume of Earth. Besides its famous 'rings', formed by countless icy particles reflecting the dim sunlight, Saturn is celebrated for the number of its moons. There are ten in all, and the largest, Titan, is the biggest satellite in the solar system. Larger than the planet Mercury, it has its own cloudy atmosphere of hydrogen and methane. It was on Titan that the Earthmen had built their refuelling base. Giant fans sucked the hydrogen/methane atmosphere through enormous intake shafts, into the station's storage tanks where it was processed and converted into chemical booster fuel. The station itself was bleakly functional, its machinery and living quarters embedded deep in solid rock. It was a place of winding tunnels and metal corridors festooned with miles of sprawling gas-pipes. Here the crew of the shuttle craft were to live, or at least exist, for the next six months, relieving the three-man crew already there.

The space shuttle drifted into the station docking bay and locked on, the whole operation master-minded by the computer. There was a clang and a hiss as the ship's airlock connected with the tunnel that led into the base.

In the control cabin the computer said, 'Docking complete. Ship locked-on.'

The three crewmen were pulling on their helmets and space gauntlets, moving in uncanny unison, as though under the direction of a single mind. Safran went over to the arms locker, and took out three hand-blasters. He passed two to Meeker and Silvey, and kept the third for himself. He slipped the blaster into the thigh-pocket of his space-suit and the others did the same.

Safran led them to the airlock door and swung it open.

They moved through the little tunnel, Safran opened another door and they emerged into a metal corridor.

A cheerful voice came from a near-by loudspeaker. 'Are we glad to see you! Welcome to Titan—and you're welcome to it!' The voice paused as if expecting some answer. Safran, Meeker and Silvey stood motionless, waiting. The only sound was the strangely hoarse breathing from beneath their helmets. After a moment, the voice went on, 'Well, we're all in the mess, celebrating. Come and join us.'

The corridor led to a wider one, broader and better lit, and that in turn led to an open area with two metal doors. One was marked Crew Mess Room. From behind it came laughter and a babble of cheerful talk. The soon-to-be-relieved crew were celebrating their departure. Safran moved to the other door and opened it. Sleeping quarters, neat and empty, blankets folded, a bulging travel-pack on the end of each bunk. The Titan crew were packed and ready to go.

Safran closed the door and moved back to the mess. He drew the blaster from his pocket, and the two others did the same.

He touched a control-plate and the mess-room door slid open.

2

The Host

The departing crew were celebrating with a final dinner. Food-packs and drinks flasks littered the crew-room table. As the door opened, their captain stood up, three wine-filled beakers in his hands. 'There you are! Come on in and join the party.'

Three space-suited figures stood motionless in the doorway, their faces invisible behind dark helmet-visors. Uneasily, the captain said, 'Come on, get your gear off and relax. You're going to be here for another six ...' His voice tailed off, as Safran raised his blaster. 'Hey, what kind of a joke is ...' There was a sudden crackle of blaster-fire and the captain's body was hurled backwards. As the other crew members jumped to their feet, Meeker and Silvey shot them down. When the noise and the cries died away, three dead bodies lay sprawled across the room.

'There will be one other,' said Safran. 'The station supervisor. We must find and destroy him. Then we can make this the ideal place in which to breed and multiply.' As he spoke, Safran was taking off his helmet. A shining, metallic rash was spreading over his face, thickening the eyebrows and altering the skin around the eyes.

Meeker and Silvey showed no surprise. When they took off their helmets, the same rash was on their

16

faces too. The crew of the Titan shuttle were no longer entirely human.

The supervisor's office was the nerve centre of the base. It held lockers, a wall map of the base, and master controls for the various storage tanks.

The station supervisor's name was Lowe, and he was a fussy, methodical man. He sat in his office, nursing his injured pride. Regulations were quite specific. On arrival at the refuelling base incoming crews report to the station supervisor. Naturally enough, most stopped off for a word with the crew they were replacing. But he'd allowed plenty of time for that, and they really should be here by now.

Lowe touched the switch that would send his voice all over the base. 'Shuttle relief crew, this is Supervisor Lowe. Please report to me *immediately*.' There was no reply.

Lowe flicked irritably at the controls of the visiphone on his desk. Maybe they'd been delayed on the ship. He punched up a view of the air-lock corridor on the little screen. Empty. They must be off the ship by now. No doubt they were still drinking in the mess. Lowe switched channels—and found himself looking at a room full of dead bodies. He gave a gasp of horror. 'My God, what's happened?' With trembling fingers he fumbled at the visiphone controls. A space-suited figure appeared on the screen, walking down the corridor towards him. 'What is it?' shouted Lowe. 'What's gone wrong?'

The figure paused, then moved to the lens. Its face filled the screen. 'Wrong? There is nothing wrong.

This place is most suitable for the Purpose.'

Lowe peered at the screen. Surely that was Safran? But there was something wrong with his face, and the voice ... 'What purpose? Safran, is that you? What's happened?'

'Who is this—Safran?' asked the slurred, inhuman voice.

Horrified, Lowe switched to the corridor outside his office. Two figures were moving towards him. They had blasters in their hands, and their faces showed the same inhuman distortions as Safran.

Lowe hurried to the door and locked it. He opened a panel in his desk to reveal a high-powered space radio, and pressed a red button marked 'Distress Call'. The transmitter started giving out a high-pitched, urgent beep. 'Mayday, Mayday, Mayday,' said Lowe urgently. 'This is Titan Base. Mayday, Mayday, Mayday.' He switched the transmitter to record and repeat, crossed to a locker and took out an emergency space suit. He pulled the locker away from the wall, revealing a circular hatch. Quickly Lowe began climbing into the suit.

Silvey and Meeker reached the door to the supervisor's office minutes later. They tried it, found it locked, turned their blasters on the lock. There was a fierce crackle of energy and the locking device melted away. They kicked the door open and burst into the room—just in time to see the emergency escape hatch close. They ran to the thick plastiglass window, but saw only the drifting clouds of gas and the blackness of space beyond ...

Meeker turned as Safran came into the room. 'The supervisor has escaped.'

Safran considered. The part of his mind that was still human knew that the emergency suits and escape hatches were intended for use in case of some localised disaster, to enable station crew to reach a rescue ship. The built-in back-pack carried only a very limited oxygen supply. 'Leave him. Let him suffocate.'

The bleeping of the distress signal was still filling the room, Safran went to the set and switched it off. The bleeping died away and he leaned over the transmitter. 'Titan Base, this is Titan Base to all vessels. Disregard Mayday.'

The TARDIS hung suspended in space, waiting for the Doctor to decide on its new destination.

A cloud appeared, and began drifting towards the TARDIS. As it approached it seemed to grow bigger and more dense ...

Leela waited patiently while the Doctor made minute adjustments to the TARDIS programme-circuits. Sensing her boredom, the Doctor said, 'Shan't be long, Leela. As soon as I've finished these checks we'll go somewhere really interesting.'

Suddenly there was a high-pitched beep and a voice crackled from the TARDIS console. 'Mayday, Mayday, Mayday, this is Titan Base ... Mayday, Mayday, Mayday, this is Titan Base.' The same message, repeated over and over.

The Doctor flicked a switch, and the transmission was cut off. He stood up, frowning at the console.

'What was that?' asked Leela curiously.

'Distress call from Titan. Took a while to reach us.'

'Is Titan really interesting?'

'What does that matter?' snapped the Doctor. 'What's important is that someone needs help.' He began re-programming the TARDIS.

Leela sighed. Sometimes it seemed she could never say the right thing.

The space cloud had drifted very close to the TARDIS by now. It pulsed with energy and something gleamed and flickered in its depths ...

Leela shivered.

The Doctor stopped muttering incomprehensible calculations to himself and looked up. 'What's the matter, Leela?'

'I am troubled.'

'What about?'

'I don't know. I can—*feel* something.'

'Don't worry,' said the Doctor vaguely, and went on with his work.

Urgent beeping filled the control room once again, and a voice came from the console speaker. It was a different voice this time, with something slurred and dragging about it. 'Titan—this is Titan Base. All vessels, repeat, all vessels, disregard Mayday. I say again, disregard Mayday. All under control. Our apologies, our apologies. Titan Base out.'

'That's it!' said Leela suddenly.

'That's what?'

'That voice. It was something evil. It was not a human voice, like the first one.'

'It wasn't?' The Doctor stared at her in astonishment. He opened his mouth to speak—then suddenly went rigid . . .

As the TARDIS brushed the fringes of the drifting cloud, something deep within flared into life, lashing out with a lightning-tentacle of energy . . .

The Doctor's body was surrounded by a kind of glowing halo. The effect faded and the Doctor shook his head and went on with his work.

Leela was astonished and alarmed. 'What was all that about, Doctor?'

'Space static. Nothing important.'

'But there was a kind of glow all round you . . .'

'There was? Probably a kind of St Elmo's fire. It happens at sea.'

'St Elmo?'

'Yes, it causes a sort of halo effect around the masts of ships.'

'Halo?'

'Why do you keep repeating everything I say?' asked the Doctor irritably. 'You're not a parrot, are you?'

'Parrot?'

'Yes. A parrot's a bird that repeats things. Move over.'

'Move over,' said Leela mischievously.

The Doctor removed another panel and stared broodingly at the inside of the console. It now seemed to be emitting a mysterious crackling.

'Is there something wrong?' asked Leela.

'There isn't actually anything *wrong*,' said the Doctor hurriedly. 'Well, nothing serious, anyway. But I shall have to check all the same.'

Leela was staring at the maze of circuitry inside the console. 'I can feel it, Doctor. Something *is* wrong ...'

The Doctor thrust his head inside the console. 'Now come on, old thing,' he said reproachfully. 'Stop acting up.' A lightning-like tentacle of energy flashed from the console and played about the Doctor's forehead. He slumped forward unconscious, his head crashing against the console. A deep throaty voice said, 'Contact has been made.'

Safran was showing his two crew-members the wall-map of Titan Base. 'We shall start the incubation process—here.' He pointed. 'One of the largest fuel tanks is empty—it will become the Hive.'

A gurgling inhuman voice spoke inside his mind. 'Contact has been made. The Nucleus has found a suitable host. Prepare for his coming ...'

With a wheezing, groaning sound the TARDIS arrived on Titan, materialising in a corridor near the airlock.

In the control room, Leela was desperately trying to revive the Doctor. 'Wake up, Doctor, we've landed. We've materialised!'

As she knelt by the Doctor, a fiery tentacle snaked from the console and played about her head. Leela didn't even notice it. 'Come on, Doctor. Wake up.'

Safran, Silvey and Meeker came running down the corridor, and waited outside the TARDIS. 'There is one other with the host,' said Safran. 'She is a reject. We must destroy her, and dispose of her body with the rest. Take up your positions.'

All three moved back out of sight, blasters covering the TARDIS door.

The Doctor opened his eyes and said, 'Hello, Lalee.'

'Doctor, are you all right?'

'Rightly perfect, thank you, Lalee,' said the Doctor solemnly.

'What did you say?'

'I said I was perfectly all right, Lalee.'

'My name is Leela.'

'I know your name,' said the Doctor indignantly. 'Leela!'

'What happened?'

The Doctor sat up, rubbing his head. 'I must have had a bot of a shick.'

'What?'

'A bot of a shick,' repeated the Doctor patiently. Suddenly his body convulsed in a kind of spasm. Leela held his shoulders, supporting him, and the attack passed as quickly as it had come.

'What is it, Doctor?'

'I'm not sure. A voice or something in my head ...'

'The evil thing!'

'Nonsense, just a nasty turn.' The Doctor climbed rather unsteadily to his feet. 'Come on, Leela, we're on Titan. Let's go and take a look around.' He strode unsteadily towards the TARDIS door, and rebounded from the edge. He paused, rubbing his shoulder. 'Odd, that . . .'

'Doctor, don't go out,' pleaded Leela.

The Doctor grasped the edge of the door to steady himself. 'What? Why not?'

Leela operated the control that closed the door.

'It's out there, waiting. Something evil. Please, Doctor, don't go!'

3
Death Sentence

Waiting in ambush, Safran and the others saw the TARDIS door open. They raised their blasters ... No one came out, and the TARDIS door closed again.

They resumed their wait. Eyes fixed on the door, they failed to see Supervisor Lowe peering through the corridor window. A few minutes later, the watching face vanished as Lowe moved away.

Out on the icy, windswept surface of Titan, Lowe groped his way through the methane fog. He worked his way round the edge of the base until he reached the emergency hatch through which he'd first emerged. With painful slowness, he opened the hatch and crawled back into the narrow tunnel.

A few minutes later, he was back in his own office. As he'd hoped, the office was empty. There only seemed to be three of his attackers, and the strange blue box was engaging their full attention.

Lowe went to his desk and took a hand-blaster from his drawer. He peered cautiously out of his office, and hurried away down the corridor.

Inside the TARDIS, the Doctor and Leela were still arguing.

'But we must go out and investigate,' insisted the Doctor. 'We've had a Mayday call.'

'No ... I can *feel* something wrong.'

'Intuition?'

'I don't care what you call it, Doctor. I knew, I knew—even before you were affected.'

'What are you talking about, affected?'

'Before you were knocked out ...'

'Leela, listen to me, I'm quite all right.' Gently but firmly the Doctor moved Leela away from the console and reached for the door control.

Blaster in hand, Lowe arrived in the corridor behind the three relief crewmen. 'Drop your weapons,' he ordered. 'I'm arresting you—all of you.'

It was a gallant attempt, but a very foolish one. Lowe was dealing with three men who didn't much care whether they lived or died, as long as they served the Purpose.

Not one of them obeyed Lowe's call to surrender. All three swung round. Silvey raised his blaster, and Lowe shot him down. Safran and Meeker opened fire, but Lowe jumped back and both missed. Before they could fire again, Lowe turned and fled down the corridor. Safran and Meeker ran in pursuit ...

Hampered by his space-suit, Lowe pounded down the metal corridors. He turned a corner and Meeker arrived in time to see the door close behind him. Meeker reached for the door control but Safran pulled him back. Anyone coming through the door would be an easy target for Lowe's blaster—and it was their duty to stay alive and carry out the Purpose.

Instead of opening the door, Safran locked it. He pointed to a wheel-valve beside the door. 'Turn off the oxygen supply.' Meeker spun the wheel and there was an abruptly cut off hiss. Safran turned away, satisfied. Lowe would suffocate or freeze.

The TARDIS door opened for the second time and the Doctor stepped out and looked around him. 'Nobody around. Not a soul.' Leela followed him from the TARDIS, her knife in her hand. The Doctor felt in his capacious pockets and found something that looked like a whistle, put it to his lips and blew hard. Unfortunately it proved to be some kind of duck lure—instead of a piercing blast, it produced only a raucous squawk. The Doctor abandoned the whistle and called loudly, 'Anyone home?'

Leela saw a foot sticking out round a near-by corner. 'Doctor, look!'

They hurried over. The body of Silvey lay sprawled where it had fallen. The Doctor stared down at it. 'Disregard Mayday,' he muttered. 'That second call we heard. He said disregard Mayday. Why?'

Leela knelt and put a hand to the dead man's neck. 'He's still warm.'

'Don't be gruesome,' said the Doctor reprovingly.

'I am a hunter ...'

'You're a savage!'

'Perhaps—I am not ashamed of what I am. And I tell you I can smell danger.'

The Doctor looked thoughtfully at her. Although

27

he often teased her about it, he had a great respect for Leela's instinct. 'Evil again, Leela?'

She nodded. 'It is everywhere in this place.'

'Then we'd better find it before it finds us. You stay here.'

The Doctor set off down the corridor. 'I am no coward,' called Leela indignantly. But the Doctor was gone. 'Stay here,' she muttered rebelliously. 'He's always telling me to stay here!' Mutinously she set off in the opposite direction.

Safran was studying the wall chart in the supervisor's office. Meeker was standing ready by the controls.

'Set temperature and humidity rate for optimum breeding conditions,' ordered Safran.

'Set temperature and humidity rate for optimum breeding conditions,' repeated Meeker obediently.

The Doctor appeared in the office doorway and watched them for a moment. He cleared his throat loudly. 'Excuse me, you don't know me. Allow me to introduce myself——'

'There is no need,' said Safran placidly. 'We are preparing the Hive now.'

'People call me the Doctor——' The Doctor broke off. 'Hive?'

'For the Nucleus which you carry within you.'

The Doctor stared at him. There was a strange metallic rash around the man's eyes, and the eyebrows were curiously thickened. 'Are you all right? I answered your Mayday . . .'

'You answered the call,' corrected Safran calmly.

'That's right. Has someone been hurt?'

'It is of no consequence. The physical envelope is of no importance.'

'Of no importance,' chorused Meeker.

'What do you mean, of no importance? I've just found a dead body out there.'

Safran came closer and stared at the Doctor. 'It is of no importance—now that you have arrived.' A jagged, lightning-like tentacle sizzled for a moment between Safran's forehead and the Doctor's, and as suddenly vanished.

'I have arrived,' said the Doctor in a slurred, dragging voice.

'All that matters is that the reject should be destroyed.'

'The reject must be destroyed.'

'And breeding begin!'

The Doctor nodded slowly. 'And breeding from *my* Nucleus begin.'

Leela crept silently along the corridor, senses alert, knife poised and ready in her hand. She was passing a closed door when she heard a faint scrabbling sound. She paused and listened. It was coming from inside the door. It took her a minute to fathom the workings of the locking mechanism, but she succeeded at last. The door slid open and a stiff, frost-covered body fell out into her arms. Leela lowered it to the ground, and knelt to check that the man was still breathing. Deciding that he was alive—just—she dragged him away.

*

The Doctor took the blaster from Safran's hand. 'Leela is a reject. She must be destroyed. She will not suspect me.'

'One of us will follow,' said Safran calmly.

'That isn't necessary . . .'

Safran ignored him. 'The Nucleus within you must not be harmed.'

'Must not be harmed,' chanted Meeker.

'Very well.'

The Doctor moved off down the corridor, blaster in hand, and Meeker followed.

Leela hauled the ice-cold body along the corridor until she reached an open door. Glancing inside she saw a room with chairs around a central table, littered with the remains of food and drink. The room also contained three dead bodies, but Leela didn't allow this to distract her. She dragged the unconscious man inside, and dropped him into a chair. The man seemed to be recovering consciousness now, and he was shivering convulsively. Leela found a plastic flask half-full of some kind of wine. She took it over to the chair and forced a few drops of wine between the man's chattering teeth. He gulped and spluttered. After a few moments he opened his eyes and looked dazedly up at her. 'Who are you?'

'We answered your Mayday. Who are you?'

'I'm Lowe—Chief Supervisor.'

'What happened here?' asked Leela.

'They tried to kill me . . . the relief crew. They're insane. They've already killed these poor devils.'

'Why? Are they your enemies?'

Lowe shook his head. 'No ... they were my friends. I know them—at least I thought I did. But they've changed.'

'Changed?'

'Their eyes, their manner, their whole behaviour is different. One of them said something ...'

'What?'

'About their purpose. "This place will be suitable for our Purpose" ... Whatever that is!'

'The Doctor will understand. He will find us soon.'

From somewhere outside a voice called, 'Leela! Leela, where are you?'

'That's him,' said Leela delightedly. 'That's the Doctor!'

She was about to call back when Lowe said, 'Wait, it could be a trap. They may have some way of taking people over.'

Leela couldn't imagine anyone controlling the Doctor, but it was as well to be cautious. 'What do you want to do?'

'Hide!'

They crouched behind an overturned bench and waited.

Blaster in hand, the Doctor moved along the corridor, Meeker close behind him. 'Don't worry, Leela,' he called. 'It's only me. Listen to me, Leela, there's nothing wrong with this place, it's most suitable. It's a good place ... a good place ...'

Leela looked worriedly at Lowe. It was the Doctor's voice all right, but there was something wrong with the tone. All the warmth and life seemed to have gone from it. And the words were strange ...

The Doctor walked along the corridor calling, 'Leela! Come on, Leela, I'm waiting!' He was quite calm. Leela was a reject and she must die. It was necessary.

Suddenly the Doctor stopped, looking at the blaster in his hand as if he had never seen it before. His own personality came flooding back and he gasped a desperate appeal to the power that had invaded his mind. 'Please leave me ... *please*! I can't do it ... I *can't* ...'

Meeker came up behind him. 'Think of the Purpose. She is a reject. She must die. Kill her!'

'I can't ...'

'Think of the Purpose. The Purpose is all important!'

Lowe shifted his position, caught an empty flask with his foot. It rolled across the floor of the mess room. It was only the tiniest sound but the Doctor heard it. His mental struggle suddenly ended as the power in his mind grew stronger. He raised his blaster and marched towards the mess room. 'The reject is here.'

Meeker paused for a moment as if listening to some silent command, then put a hand on the Doctor's shoulder. 'Stay—there is danger. The Nucleus does not wish to be harmed. *I* shall destroy her.'

'Kill her,' muttered the Doctor feverishly. 'Kill her!'

Meeker sprang through the mess-room door, firing as he came.

Lowe dodged and returned the fire. He missed, and the fringe of Meeker's blaster-bolt numbed his arm. His weapon clattered to the floor.

Meeker raised his blaster to finish him off.

Leela's knife flashed through the air and thudded into his chest. He fell back, choking . . .

In one smooth movement, Leela sprang across the room, plucked her knife from his chest, snatched the blaster from his hand and moved into the corridor.

Rubbing his arm, Lowe went over to the dying Meeker and bent over him. 'Meeker!' he whispered urgently. 'This Purpose . . . what is it?'

The dying man looked up—and smiled. A fiery tentacle of lightning flashed between his forehead and Lowe's . . .

Leela saw a huddled shape lying face down at the end of the corridor. It was the Doctor. She was hurrying towards it when she heard a voice behind her. 'Leave it to me, I know this place.' Another crewman was running along the corridor.

Leela leaped behind the shelter of a projecting massive pipe and waited in ambush.

Behind her the Doctor rolled over and raised himself on one elbow. He lifted his blaster, training it upon Leela's back. The hand that held the weapon was covered with a thick growth of coarse metallic hair.

The Doctor's finger tightened on the trigger.

4
Foundation

A deep, horribly gurgling voice spoke inside the Doctor's head. 'The reject must be destroyed. Kill the reject. *Kill it.*' Somehow the Doctor found the strength to resist. 'I can't . . .' he gasped. 'I won't.'

'You must!'

The Doctor's body convulsed, and he gave a strangled cry. 'Look out, Leela, I can't stop it.' In spite of his effort to resist, his finger pulled the trigger. But the Doctor's internal struggle had thrown off his aim. The blaster bolt passed harmlessly over Leela's head, narrowly missing Safran who was edging his way along the corridor. Safran jumped back, just as Lowe appeared in the mess-room doorway. Outnumbered, Safran turned and fled, and Lowe ran in pursuit.

The Doctor writhed on the floor, at war with himself. With a desperate effort he snatched the blaster from his own hand and threw it away from him, writhing in agony. 'Got to fight it, got to fight it,' he muttered feverishly.

Leela knelt down beside him. 'Doctor, what's happening? What was all that?'

The Doctor's face was twisted with strain. 'I'm fighting for my lives,' he whispered feebly. 'Whatever attacked the others is affecting *me*.'

'Then why doesn't it affect me?'

'Perhaps because . . .'

Another spasm shook the Doctor's body. 'I can feel it gathering strength to attack again.'

'The Evil One?'

Almost inaudibly the Doctor whispered, 'Some kind of organism that attacks the mind . . . the intelligence. It's trying to take me over, Leela.'

'No, Doctor, please . . .'

'I need help . . . I must withdraw into myself. Save strength . . .' The Doctor's head fell back, and he lapsed into a self-induced trance. Only by suspending all the functions of his body could he gain the strength he needed to fight the intruder in his mind.

Leela looked worriedly down at him. Again she murmured, 'But why not *me*?'

Lowe caught up with Safran at the airlock door. He was desperately swinging the locking wheel, and it was clear that he intended to take refuge in the shuttle craft. At the sound of Lowe's approach he swung round, blaster raised, but Lowe snapped, 'No! Contact has been made. We are one, Safran.'

Safran stared hard at him. There was a metallic rash around Lowe's eyes, and his eyebrows were beginning to thicken.

'Then why do you pursue me?'

'For the Purpose . . . The Doctor still resists the power of the Nucleus. You will stay here and prepare the tank for incubation. He does not suspect me yet. I will stay with them, to guard the Nucleus—and to destroy the reject.'

They heard light, padding footsteps coming along

the corridor. 'It is the reject,' said Lowe. He snatched a pair of space-goggles from Safran's belt and thrust the crewman to the ground.

When Leela came round the corner, Lowe was fitting the goggles over his eyes. Safran's body sprawled at his feet. Leela looked down at it. 'You got him, then?'

'Yes—but he almost got me. My eyes ... I caught the flash from his blaster.'

'You must come with me,' ordered Leela. 'The Doctor is ill, very ill. He told me to find help.'

Lowe looked worried. 'There are only the most basic medical facilities here ...'

'Where must we go then?'

They began hurrying back along the corridor to the Doctor. 'Well,' said Lowe doubtfully, 'the nearest place would be the Centre for Alien Biomorphology, the Bi-Al Foundation. It's in the asteroid belt.'

'We'll take the TARDIS,' said Leela decisively. She looked down at the Doctor, who muttered and stirred. 'Doctor, we're taking you somewhere to get help, but we'll need the TARDIS.' She turned to Lowe. '*Where* are we going?'

'It's the Bi-Al Foundation, Asteroid K4067.'

'What are the co-ordinates, Doctor?' She leaned over the Doctor and shook him. 'Doctor, what are the co-ordinates?'

The Doctor opened his eyes. 'Vector 1, 9, Quadrant 3.'

Lifting the Doctor between them, they began carrying him towards the TARDIS. Leela muttered the co-ordinates to herself. 'Vector 1, 9, Quadrant 3.' Her knowledge of technical matters was almost nil, but she had seen the Doctor take off in the TARDIS often enough. Moreover, the Doctor had instructed her in basic takeoff and landing procedures, saying she might need the information in some emergency.

Now that emergency had arrived. As she lifted the TARDIS key from round the Doctor's neck, Leela hoped desperately that she could remember what she'd been told. It looked as if the Doctor's life depended on it.

The Bi-Al Foundation was one of the largest and most impressive research hospitals in the galaxy, occupying almost the entire centre of the huge, hollowed-out asteroid. Set up by a number of business conglomerates back on Earth, it was ideally placed to deal with the frequent injuries and many strange ailments encountered by the explorers who passed through the asteroid belt on their way to the outer planets.

The Foundation's thousands of gleaming windows shone brilliantly out into the blackness of space, level upon level of them. Embedded in the centre of the building was an enormous glowing red cross, symbol of the healer since the earliest days of Man.

They were used to strange craft and strange travellers at the Bi-Al Foundation. Once the staff had recovered from the shock of the TARDIS materialisation in main reception, they were treated like any other space travellers. White-clad nurses lifted the Doctor on to a trolley, and carried him to a lift, which whisked him out of sight with a pneumatic whoosh.

Leela and Lowe were left at the reception desk, where an icily efficient lady sat in the midst of an array of communication devices. Leela looked uneasily around her. Long white corridors radiated off from this central area. There were bustling doctors and nurses in their different coloured robes, huddled patients waiting on their benches. Although she didn't know it, this was a basic hospital scene that hadn't changed for thousands of years.

The receiving officer was looking at her impatiently. fingers poised over the computer terminal in-put keys. 'Patient's name?'

'Er—he's just called the Doctor.'

'Place of origin?'

'Gallifrey.'

'That's Earth, isn't it? Ireland?'

'I expect so.'

'Thank you, that's all we need for now.'

'But where is he?'

'Level X_4, Isolation.'

The receiving officer touched a control, and a monitor screen showed the Doctor lying on a bed, surrounded by a complex array of automated diagnostic instruments. 'He's being datalysed.'

'Being what?' asked Leela, alarmed.

'Treatment is already under way,' said the receptionist with professional reassurance. 'Are you next of kin?'

'Oh ... yes. I don't know. I expect so.'

Lowe came up to the reception desk. 'Where's the Doctor?'

'They've taken him away,' said Leela helplessly. 'To level X_4.'

'X_4?'

'Isolation wing,' repeated the nurse briskly. She

looked at Lowe's goggled face. 'And what's your trouble?'

'Blaster flash—it was an accident.'

The receptionist pointed. 'Eye section, straight through, they'll deal with you there.'

Lowe nodded to Leela. 'I'll find you later, then.' He hurried away.

'Can I see the Doctor?' asked Leela hopefully.

'Not until Professor Marius has examined him.'

'Marius?'

'He's our specialist in extra-terrestrial pathological endomorphisms,' said the receptionist proudly. Then her manner became formal again. 'Will you wait there please?'

She pointed to a row of seats. Leela sat down to wait.

The Doctor lay unconscious on a bed in the isolation ward. Standing over him was Professor Marius, a stocky Germanic figure, whose comfortable, informal clothes indicated that he was too senior to be bothered with looking respectable. An explosively cheerful professor from New Heidelberg University, Marius had come to the asteroid belt in search of new and rare diseases. So far he had come up with nothing sufficiently exotic to satisfy him.

Hovering beside the bed were Parsons, Marius's keen young assistant, and his senior nurse. Also included in the little group was the squat metallic creature that stood near the bottom of the bed. It looked curiously like a kind of squared-off metal dog, with a computer display screen for eyes, and antennae for ears and tail. At the moment it was studying the

Doctor's motionless form with a very sophisticated battery of scanning devices. A strip of computer-print-out papers began sprouting from its mouth, rather like a very long tongue.

When the print-out strip stopped protruding itself, Marius leaned down, patted the metal creature on the head, and tore off the strip.

He studied it for a moment and then looked up at his two assistants. 'Blithering idiots!' he said witheringly.

Doctor Parsons and the Nurse exchanged glances and said nothing. They were used to Professor Marius.

'This man is in a self-induced coma,' continued Marius. 'There's absolutely nothing wrong with the fellow. Look at him—he's probably one of these good-for-nothing spaceniks!' Descendants of the hippies and beatniks of the late twentieth century, spaceniks were penniless wanderers who somehow managed to smuggle themselves on board various kinds of space craft in their desire to commune with the mysteries of the universe. Since they were without either financial resources or technical skills, they usually landed in trouble, and had to be ferried home by the Terrestrial Government at enormous expense.

Marius looked disgustedly at the untidy specimen before him. 'Why have I been sent for? Tell me that —why? It's a complete and utter waste of my valuable time!'

With a kind of electronic growl, K9 produced another data strip. Parsons studied it. 'Excuse me, sir.'

'What is it now?'

'K9 indicates that this patient is not a member of the human race.'

Marius turned. 'Nonsense. Just look at him.'

'See for yourself, sir,' insisted Parsons. He passed Marius the data strip. 'Two hearts and a self-renewing cell structure.'

Marius looked down. 'Is that right, K9?'

The little creature spoke in a gruff metallic voice. 'Affirmative, Master.'

Marius examined the Doctor with a good deal more interest. 'Non-human, is he? Point of origin?'

'Beyond the solar system.'

With heavy sarcasm, Marius said, 'Thank you, K9.'

'Master,' said the metal dog smugly. Irony was wasted on automatons.

Marius turned to the nurse, 'Let's get an encephalograph out on him, eh?'

The nurse reached for a complex piece of equipment on a flexible arm, and swung it close to the Doctor's head.

K9 transmitted the results. 'Unidentified viral-type infection with noetic characteristics. At present seated in the mind-brain interface, and therefore having no ascertainable mass or structure—Master.'

Marius rubbed his hands. 'Interesting! Most interesting! Not every day we discover a brand-new infection, eh. Parsons?'

'No, sir,' said Parsons dutifully.

The Doctor opened his eyes. 'Hello!' he said cheerfully.

Marius was delighted. 'Good evening!'

The Doctor looked at the maze of electronic equipment surrounding his bed 'Find anything?'

'Not yet, my boy, but we will!' Marius looked at the chart at the bottom of the Doctor's bed. 'You're a Doctor, I see.'

'That's right. Come on now, what have you found?'

'Cataleptic trance?' suggested Marius.

'Yes.'

'Self-induced?'

'Yes.'

'Why?'

'Self-preservation,' said the Doctor simply. 'Whatever it is I'm suffering from seems to thrive on mental activity.'

Marius was fascinated. 'I see ... so the harder you think, the more of a grip it seems to take?'

'That's right. Non-thinking is the only way to shake it off—but I can't stay mindless for eternity, can I?'

'Take your point, take your point,' mumbled Marius sympathetically. 'Now, my computer here ...'

The Doctor looked down and seemed quite unsurprised to see a robot dog at the end of his bed. 'Hello, old chap, good dog!'

'Hullo!' said K9 politely.

'And how are you?'

Before K9 could reply, Marius cut firmly through these social exchanges. 'As I was saying, Doctor, K9 seems to think that the virus is noetic in character—which means it would only be detectable during consciousness.'

'I know what noetic means,' said the Doctor irritably.

'I'm sorry.'

The Doctor waved the apology aside. 'So, the virus is somewhere in the mind-brain interface?'

Marius shrugged. 'If it exists ...'

The Doctor was caught up in his own deductions. 'Of course, how stupid. That's why it attacked the TARDIS computer first, because it was showing the greatest amount of mental activity. I was just idling, so to speak ...'

'When was this?'

'When we were first attacked, on our way to Titan. I assumed it was just a static build-up. And then when I checked the computer it jumped into my mind—and that explains why Leela was unaffected. Have you met Leela? She's all instinct and intuition. That's why the virus rejected her. Of course, I can see it all now!'

'It's possible, possible,' said Marius, who didn't really see at all. A thought struck him. 'Was anyone else exposed to this virus of yours?'

'Yes, the entire crew on Titan succumbed to it— with one exception, a man called Lowe. He came here with us ...'

'Supervisor Lowe is in the eye section,' volunteered K9. He was linked to the main hospital computer and knew most of what went on.

'Are you sure?' snapped Marius.

'Affirmative.' As always when his answers were questioned, there was a slightly huffy note in K9's voice.

Marius turned to the Doctor. 'Are you sure that this man Lowe was exposed——'

He broke off. The Doctor was lying back motionless, eyes closed. Feeling the alien force in his mind gather-

43

ing strength, struggling to lash out and take over Marius and the others, the Doctor had returned to his trance, determined to starve it of the mental energy upon which it fed.

'Oh, he's gone again,' said Marius disappointedly. 'I want him kept under constant observation. Full monitoring. See to it, K9.'

'Affirmative, Master.'

Marius turned to his assistant. 'We'd better get hold of this chap Lowe and take a look at him. Even if he wasn't affected, he could still be a carrier . . .'

Supervisor Lowe was sitting in an examination chair with an eye specialist standing over him. 'How did this happen?'

'An accident—on Titan.'

'What sort of accident?'

Lowe didn't reply. The specialist sighed. 'Well, let's have a look at you . . .'

'Certainly,' said Lowe. He lifted the goggles from his eyes, and a sudden lightning-streak flashed between his forehead and that of the doctor.

The specialist staggered back, hand to his eyes. When he lowered the hand a second later, his face was quite calm.

In a slurred, dragging voice he said, 'Contact has been made.'

5
Counter-attack

It didn't take Leela very long to get bored, sitting in the reception area waiting for news. She'd never been one to pay much attention to the orders of authority. Choosing a moment when the receptionist was busy, Leela slipped out of her seat, and went to look for the Doctor.

She'd memorised the only clue she had to his whereabouts—level X4—and there were plenty of signs to follow. There were plenty of people moving along the white corridors, specialists striding in solitary majesty, chattering groups of medical students, nurses murmuring quietly together. One or two people glanced curiously at her, but the Bi-Al Foundation was used to strange visitors. No one made any attempt to stop her, or ask her where she was going.

Distrusting the high-speed lift, Leela reached level X4 by climbing endless flights of service stairs. When she reached level X4 at last, she found herself in another complex of white corridors, though these were silent and empty.

She saw a door ahead of her marked 'Isolation Wing. Strictly No Admittance', and promptly opened it.

Behind it she found the Doctor, stretched out on a kind of couch, surrounded by an array of instruments. 'Doctor!' said Leela delightedly.

To her astonishment, a kind of robot animal glided from the other side of the couch and began barking orders at her. 'Negative, negative, negative, no entry!'

Leela had no intention of being chased away now she'd found the Doctor at last. Her hand went to the blaster thrust into her belt. 'Look, you—whatever-you-are ...'

'I am K9,' interrupted the little creature importantly, 'and I am warning you ...'

Leela drew her blaster. 'Look, I came to see the Doctor—I *arrived* with him.'

K9 ignored the explanation, his attention focused on Leela's blaster. 'I too have offensive capability,' he said proudly. A stubby blaster-muzzle protruded from just under his nose. 'You have been warned. Retreat, retreat!' K9 glided menacingly towards Leela. 'Patient in total isolation. Contagion risk. Retreat, retreat!'

Leela backed away—and bumped straight into the stocky figure of Professor Marius, who was just coming through the door behind her. 'Who are you?'

'I am Leela.'

'Ah, yes, of course. The Doctor's aide?'

'I think so.'

Marius looked down at his bristling companion. 'K9, memorise. Friend.'

The muzzle of K9's blaster retracted. 'Memorised. Friend.'

'Is that tin thing something to do with you?' demanded Leela.

Marius was indignant. 'That tin thing is my best friend and constant companion. He's a computer!' Leela looked bemused and Marius explained. 'You see, on Earth I always used to have a dog. But up

46

here, with the weight penalty, well, it's just not possible. So I had K9 made up. He's very useful, my own personal data bank. Knows everything I know, don't you, K9?'

'Affirmative—and more—Master!'

Ignoring this bit of robotic conceit, Marius went over to his patient. 'I'm afraid there's not much I can tell you about the Doctor yet.' He looked appraisingly at Leela. 'You know, I should like to have you scanned and datalysed.' Leela backed away in some alarm. 'Just to see why you're immune. You see, if we can isolate that factor, we can inoculate against it. Do you understand me?'

'I'm sorry,' said Leela blankly.

Marius looked thoughtfully at her. 'Yes, perhaps the Doctor was right. Maybe it is all a matter of intelligence . . .'

Parsons came hurrying into the room, and Marius said sharply, 'Well, what about this Lowe chap? Where is he?'

'He *was* in the eye section, sir, but he's disappeared. The consultant seems to have vanished as well . . .'

A trolley was being wheeled slowly along the hospital corridors. Lowe lay stretched out on it, and the trolley was being pushed by the eye consultant who had attempted to treat him.

Two young doctors appeared, walking towards them. 'Who are they?' hissed Lowe.

'Doctors. Cruickshank and Hedges.'

'Get them over here.'

The consultant raised his voice. 'Cruickshank,

Hedges, interesting eye-case here. Come and have a look!'

Unsuspectingly, the two young doctors wandered over. Cruickshank bent over to look at the patient. Hedges suddenly became aware that the consultant was staring at him with strange intensity. 'What is it?'

'Now!' hissed Lowe.

A jagged lightning-streak flashed between the foreheads of Lowe and Cruickshank, Hedges and the consultant. Slowly the two doctors straightened up. 'Contact has been made,' said Cruickshank, in a slurred dragging voice.

In exactly the same tone, Hedges said, 'Contact has been made.'

Lowe sat up, and swung his legs down from the trolley. 'A place has been found, most suitable for our purpose. Titan is being prepared as a Hive. Meanwhile our duty here is twofold. To guard the Nucleus, which is in the mind of one called Doctor, and to make contact with the best minds here. When we leave for incubation on Titan, all rejects will be destroyed.'

The consultant studied the two new servants of the Purpose. 'Do you understand?'

'We understand,' said Cruikshank.

'Contact must be made,' said Hedges.

Reverently Lowe whispered, 'For the Purpose!'

Leela lay apprehensively on a couch, being scanned by a complex of instruments similar to that surrounding the Doctor. Marius, Parsons, and a nurse stood over her. K9 waited at the foot of the bed, ready to convey the results of the scan.

'Virus contamination would seem to be complete and total,' Marius was saying in his best lecturer's voice. 'If there is anything unique in her metabolism that enables her to resist, the scanner will detect it.'

Lights flashed, instruments buzzed, clicked and whirred. At last K9 said, 'Negative on immunity, Master.'

'But there must be *something*!'

Parsons looked doubtful. 'But what if there isn't, sir?'

Marius looked over at the couch that held the Doctor. 'Then he's our only guinea-pig, the only one to be affected by the disease and yet be able to resist it.' Marius came to a decision. 'I can't allow him to be taken over like those poor devils on Titan. If there's no immunity factor in Leela—I will have to operate on the Doctor!'

Lowe and his three new recruits were walking steadily along the corridors, when suddenly Lowe stopped dead. He went rigid, a hand to his forehead. 'Contact!'

A throaty, gurgling voice spoke inside Lowe's head. 'I am endangered ...'

Reverently Lowe said, 'It is the Nucleus ...'

'The host is threatened ...' said the gurgling, inhuman voice.

Lowe listened for a moment longer then turned to the others. 'The Nucleus says that the Doctor, its host, is in danger. We must act before it is too late. Now, all of you—concentrate.'

The captain of the Bi-Al supply shuttle sat relaxed

in his command chair, his two crew members dozing in their acceleration couches behind him. They would soon be approaching Asteroid K4067, and the computer would carry out the simple docking manoeuvre with its usual efficiency ... Everything was routine ...

Outside, in the blackness of space, a drifting, formless cold had appeared from nowhere, materialising directly in the path of the shuttle. As the shuttle passed through it, lightning streaked from the cloud and played about the ship ...

Suddenly the shuttle captain noticed that the ship was increasing speed. It was boosting to maximum power-drive—and heading straight for the asteroid.

Panic-stricken, he tried to switch the controls to manual. Lightning tentacles flashed from the computer keyboard and played over his head and those of the two dozing crewmen. The shuttle captain sat back in his chair, watching calmly as his ship hurtled towards certain disaster. Contact had been made— for the Purpose. Everything was in order ...

It took some time to prepare the Doctor for his brain operation. Marius insisted on taking scan after scan of the Doctor's brain, and he made all his preparations with agonising care. He knew that the operation was a last desperate hope, and that there was a chance the Doctor would not survive it.

Marius accepted the responsibility unflinchingly, for

he knew the alternatives. Either the Doctor would become the slave of the alien force in his mind, or he would remain, in his own words, mindless for all eternity.

The Doctor was ready at last. Robed and masked, Marius and Parsons leaned over him as he lay on the operating table. K9 waited to monitor the operation. Leela hovered uneasily by the door, not wanting to stay, yet unwilling to leave the Doctor.

In a calm, steady voice, Marius was giving his final instructions. 'No anaesthetics yet, Parsons, he's still in the self-induced trance. K9, monitor the brain. If he shows signs of emerging from the coma, warn me at once, otherwise the shock might kill him.'

'Affirmative, Master.'

Marius leaned forward, ready to make the first delicate insertion of the laser micro-probe into the Doctor's brain. A voice blared from the speaker. 'Emergency, emergency! All stations, all stations, emergency. Supply shuttle approaching base on collision course, apparently out of control, refusing to respond to signals. All medical personnel report to casualty at once. Repeat, all medical personnel.'

Marius lowered the scalpel with a groan of protest. 'Now? Why now?'

For a moment he considered continuing with the operation, then abandoned the idea. He could scarcely carry out a delicate brain-operation with the entire base in chaos. Besides, it was impossible to predict what damage the collision might cause. An interruption in power supplies for instance would be literally fatal.

'Repeat, emergency, emergency!' said the speaker

voice. 'All medical personnel to casualty immediately.'

'We'll have to go, sir,' said Parsons despairingly.

'Yes, yes, I know we have to go. K9, stay in charge here. No one is to come into contact with him. Have you got that? No one!'

'Affirmative!'

'Well, come along, Parsons,' roared Marius, and rushed from the room, Parsons trailing behind him.

Leela stood looking anxiously down at the Doctor. His face was calm and still. There was no sign that he was still alive.

The supply shuttle screamed out of space and crashed into the side of the Bi-Al building. Debris shot upwards and floated away. Masonry, equipment and people too were sucked into space as the damaged sections depressurised.

The shuttle embedded itself deep into the side of the building—but not at random. The point of impact had been precisely calculated . . .

There was a shattering thud, cries, screams, the shriek of tortured metal and plastic. The whole room shook, lights flickered and then came on again. Leela staggered, fighting to keep her balance. The shock of the impact woke the Doctor up. He opened his eyes and said peevishly, 'What's that?'

Leela got to her feet. 'There's been some kind of accident—a shuttle crashed. They've all gone to help.'

'Where did it hit?'

It was K9 who answered. 'On level X3 below. As a

result of structural damage this area is now cut off.'

The Doctor sat up. 'What?' he shouted.

Lowe and his three helpers ran along a corridor, and found their way completely blocked by fallen rubble. Lowe turned to the consultant. 'We have to get to level X4. There must be other ways.'

'We could try the service shaft—but it would take longer.'

'Then *hurry*!' snarled Lowe.

The consultant led them away.

The voice from the speaker said, 'All available personnel to accident zone on level X3, repeat, level X3.'

The Doctor seemed to have recovered, at least for the moment. 'I don't think that was an accident.'

'Why not?' asked Leela.

'It must be something to do with whatever's in my head,' said the Doctor positively. 'K9, could I have a word with you?'

'Affirmative.'

Leela began edging towards the door, and the Doctor said, 'Where are you off to?'

'I think I'm needed out here.'

Leela slipped out of the room and stationed herself just outside the isolation ward door, drawing her blaster. She didn't completely understand what was going on—but she had a well-developed instinct for approaching danger. If the accident had been planned to isolate them, as the Doctor seemed to think, it could mean only one thing—their enemies were about to attack. Pleased to be faced with a problem she could understand and deal with, Leela drew her blaster and waited ...

Inside the isolation ward the Doctor was saying impatiently, 'Cloning techniques, K9! Give me a rundown, state of the art so far ...'

K9 liked nothing better than to be asked for some of his ample store of scientific information. He gave a sudden beep, the robotic equivalent of clearing his throat. 'Cloning is a form of replication, making a copy of an individual using a single cell of that individual as a matrix. Clones retain characteristics of original organism.'

'Go on, go on!' said the Doctor urgently.

'Successful experiments first carried out in the year thirty-nine, twenty-two.'

'Thirty-nine, twenty-two. Good, good! Carry on.'

K9 continued his lecture. 'More recently, the development of the Kilbracken technique of rapid holograph-cloning ...'

The Doctor listened, his mind racing. He was beginning to form a plan ... a plan that would enable him to fight back at the strange force that threatened to take him over. He had very little time ...

6

The Clones

The end of the corridor was totally blocked by a twisted mass of metal—the remains of the shuttle-craft that had embedded itself into the foundation. Surrounded by members of his rescue squad, the faithful Parsons at his side, Marius was examining two shattered bodies that had been recovered from the wreckage. Both had curiously thickened eyebrows and a metallic rash about the eyes.

Marius straightened up, his face grave. 'If these two unfortunates have contracted the virus, we must assume that they all have. If we attempt further rescue and treatment, the disease could spread like wildfire and wipe out the entire Foundation.' He waved the rescue squad away. 'Everybody back. Clear the area. Everybody out of here!' He turned to the head of the squad. 'I want the whole area cryogenically cocooned until we find out more about the nature of this virus. Get out the helium pumps. Parsons, nurse, come with me, we must attend to the Doctor!'

Other people had plans for the Doctor, too. Lowe and his three aides were creeping towards the door of the isolation ward. They had broken into a security-locker, and now all four were armed with blasters.

Lowe was in the lead. He edged round a corner—and found himself facing Leela, blaster in hand. Mutually astonished, both fired at the same time. Both missed.

'Destroy her,' screamed Lowe. 'That's the reject.'

'Reject yourself,' shouted Leela, and sent another blaster-bolt sizzling towards his head. Lowe ducked back just in time. He and the others found cover and began shooting back. Soon blaster-bolts were sizzling up and down the corridor.

In the middle of it all Marius and Parsons came running along the corridor from the other direction, followed by Marius's nurse. Leela yelled over her shoulder, 'It's Lowe—he's got the disease! Get inside, I'll cover you.'

The three leaped inside the isolation ward where K9 was just concluding his lecture. 'At present, holographic-cloning technique is simple but unreliable.'

'Hurry, K9, hurry!'

Rapidly speeding up his delivery K9 gabbled, 'Holographic replicas do not maintain their existence because of possible unsolved psychic problems.'

'How long, how long?' demanded the Doctor.

'Longest recorded life, ten minutes.'

'Ten minutes fifty-five seconds,' corrected Marius.

The Doctor looked up eagerly. 'Professor Marius, could you clone me?'

Marius shrugged. 'Certainly. The Kilbracken technique is almost absurdly simple. But it's a circus trick, no medical value.'

'Could you clone me now?'

'Now?'

'Yes. Because if you don't clone me now, and the virus gets to me, it'll take the whole Centre over.'

Leela fired off a final volley of blaster-bolts. The last one fizzled out in a dispirited whine. She ducked back inside the ward. 'Can't hold them off any longer, out of ammunition.'

'K9!' snapped Marius. 'Kalaylee!'

'Affirmative, Master!'

'What does that mean?'

Marius smiled grimly. 'He knows!'

Blaster-muzzle projecting, K9 trundled out into the corridor like a small canine tank. He blazed away at the attackers, who were rushing forwards, confident of victory. His first shot blasted down the astonished Hedges. Lowe and the others turned and fled. When they were safe round the corner, Lowe paused. 'We'll never get past them that way. Is there a visiphone?'

'In my office,' said the consultant. They hurried away.

Marius and his nurse were supervising the installation of a portable booth with opaque plastic sides, not un-like a twentieth-century telephone kiosk. A tiny control panel was set into one side. 'Hurry, Marius, hurry!' urged the Doctor. His brief spell of recovery seemed to be coming to an end, and he was weakening rapidly. Deep in his mind, the dormant virus was struggling to reassert its control.

Marius checked circuit-connections, and waved the technicians away. He went over to the Doctor, lifted a scalpel from an instrument-tray held by his nurse and took a minute sample of the Doctor's skin.

'You must realise, Doctor, that this will not be, in any real sense a clone but a short-lived carbon-based imprint, a sort of living, three-dimensional photograph.'

The Doctor's strength was fading rapidly. 'Leela,' he muttered. 'I shall need Leela ...' He fell back, unconscious.

Leela checked the blaster she'd taken from Hedges's body. 'What did he mean, he needs me?'

'It must be because you are immune. I think he wants you cloned as well.'

Marius picked up his scalpel and reached for Leela's hand.

'But what will happen to me, the real me?'

'Nothing. Nothing at all,' said Marius soothingly.

'But you said it was just short-lived.'

Marius transferred his skin sample into the special cloning dish and added the necessary nutrient solutions, talking as he worked. 'A permanent clone or copy is theoretically possible, but it would take years to achieve because of the experiential gap.' He carried the containers over to the booth. 'Now in this way we manage to transfer both heredity and experience, but the transfer is unstable ...'

'What does that mean?'

Marius sighed. 'It means that your photo-copy twin will deteriorate and vanish after a maximum life of ten or eleven minutes.'

Leela felt it would be rather unpleasant, watching yourself fade away and disappear. 'Oh, I see,' she said politely. 'Then in that case I don't think I'll stay to see her. If you need me I shall be with K9.'

'Yes, yes, yes,' said Marius impatiently, and carried the first cloning dish over to the booth. He nodded to

Parsons, who switched on the machine. There was a hum of power and a steadily rising beep. The booth was flooded with dazzling light, and inside the radiance a shape began to form ...

It cohered, solidified, and seconds later the Doctor stepped out of the booth. The second self was identical to the Doctor on the couch—the Kilbracken technique had reproduced every detail, including clothing. The new Doctor nodded briefly to Marius and headed for the door.

'Doctor, where are you going?'

The new Doctor turned. 'Trust me, Professor Marius, just trust me.' He disappeared through the door.

Marius sighed. 'I hope he knows what he's doing. Come along, Parsons, we'd better get on with cloning the girl.' He picked up the second cloning dish and carried it over to the booth.

Leela, the real Leela, looked up in astonishment when the Doctor, apparently restored to full health, came out of the ward and strode briskly down the corridor.

Staring after his disappearing figure she asked, 'Which one was that?'

K9's sensors enabled him to differentiate between original and carbon copy. 'That was the Doctor-2.'

'Can you explain?'

'Affirmative.'

'Well?'

'The Kilbracken holograph-cloning technique replicates from a single cell a short-lived carbon copy. Efficacy of individuation not completely guaranteed.'

'Can you explain *simply*?'

'Negative!' said K9.

The consultant led Lowe and Cruickshank into the eye section—and straight into one of the consultant's students, who looked curiously at them. 'Come here,' snapped the consultant. The student came over to them. Lightning sizzled between the consultant's forehead and his own . . .

The cloned version of Leela stood fully formed inside the booth. Marius was about to release her when he heard a horrified cry from his nurse. 'Professor Marius —look at the Doctor!'

Marius turned. While they had been busy, the virus had taken over the Doctor's body with horrifying speed. The entire shape seemed twisted and distorted, and a rash of wiry metallic hairs had grown over his hands and face. It was as though the Doctor were turning into some strange deformed beast before their eyes. His entire body was twisting, writhing, convulsing with such force that Marius feared he would break a limb. He fetched heavy plastic restraining webbing from a locker, and he and Parsons fought to strap the struggling figure down.

As they fought with him the Doctor began to speak, not in his own voice, but in deep, throaty, gurgling inhuman tones, that sounded like someone choking on his own blood. 'Release this body,' gurgled the voice. 'You cannot prevail. I am the One. It is my Purpose. It is my destiny. *Let me go, you fools!*'

'Shall we sedate him?' asked Parsons.

Marius fastened the last buckle with a mighty effort. 'No. Not yet.'

'What about the danger of contagion?'

'No, Parsons. If the disease was contagious during this stage, we would all have got it by now.'

Parsons looked down at the writhing figure. 'If the Doctor's right, sir, and the virus is intelligent, it must have some reason for choosing him.'

'That's right. In my view, we could be dealing with some kind of leader.'

The horrifying voice came from the Doctor's twisted mouth once more. 'My Purpose. You must not delay my Purpose. The place of the Hive is ready. Release me!'

The TARDIS doors opened and the carbon-copy Doctor emerged carrying a complex piece of electronic equipment. Clasping it to his chest, he hurried off down the corridor.

The visiphone screen in the isolation ward suddenly lit up and Lowe appeared on the screen. The rash had spread all over his face now, and like the Doctor he seemed scarcely human. 'Professor Marius, listen to me,' he said menacingly. 'You must release the Doctor.'

Marius struggled to hold down the writhing figure on the couch. 'Never,' he gasped defiantly.

'I warn you, we are in control of the entire Centre.

We have made contact with your atomic generator technicians. If you do not do as I say, I shall destroy your Foundation!'

Waiting in the corridor with K9, Leela saw the Doctor hurrying towards them clutching a heavy piece of equipment, which she recognised as part of the TARDIS console. He marched straight past them and into the isolation ward.

'That was the Doctor-2,' said Leela definitely.

'Affirmative!'

As the second Doctor came into the ward, Lowe was still uttering threats from the visiphone screen. 'You have two minutes in which to decide. Either you give us the Doctor or your Foundation will be wiped out!' The screen went dark.

The Doctor was carrying his piece of equipment over to the cloning booth.

Marius followed him. 'What are you doing, Doctor? Didn't you hear? We've just had an ultimatum.'

'Don't worry, Professor, if this doesn't work the whole place will be wiped out anyway.'

Marius stared at the machinery. 'What is it?'

'It's a Relative Dimensional Stabiliser, RDS.'

'What does it do?'

'It's part of the TARDIS control system, the part that allows me to cross the dimensional barriers.'

Marius looked blank. The Doctor said, 'It's quite simple, really. It means that I can change size, large or small as I wish.' He opened the door to the booth, and found himself facing an angry carbon-copy Leela. 'Why have I been left here?'

'Sorry, Leela, shan't keep you a minute.' The new Doctor began setting up the RDS inside the booth. 'Now listen carefully, Professor. I'll operate the RDS. I've set it so that we'll be reduced to micro-dimensions. You then scoop us both up and inject us into my master-print, there.' He nodded briefly at the figure on the couch. 'When we return, you simply throw the RDS in reverse to restore us to normal size. This lever here ... Any questions?'

Marius had only one. 'Why take Leela?'

'Because she's immune—and because she's a hunter!'

'Yes, of course. Well, we'd better get on with it, there's not much time. Is there anything we can do meanwhile?'

'Yes, just stay here and hope we come up with the antidote. And Professor, when we emerge, we'll be coming out through the tear duct!'

'Right. Good luck!'

The carbon-copy Doctor stepped inside the booth with the carbon-copy Leela.

Meanwhile the original Leela, overcome by curiosity, was watching from the doorway. She caught a glimpse of her carbon copy through the open door of the booth. 'K9, do I really look like that?'

'Affirmative.'

There was a hum of power from inside the booth and the dim shapes of the Doctor and Leela dwindled rapidly to nothingness.

Marius waited a moment longer, then opened the door. The booth was empty except for the little dish of serum in the centre of the floor. Marius picked it up carefully, and his nurse handed him a specially prepared pneumatic syringe. Marius sucked up the few drops of colourless fluid in the dish and carried the syringe over to the couch. He looked at Parsons. 'Well, here they go!' He bent over the couch. 'Pleasant journey, Doctor,' he whispered, and injected the fluid into the back of the Doctor's neck.

Lowe's face appeared on the visiphone screen. 'Your time is up,' he said harshly. 'Surrender the Doctor!'

Carbon-copied and miniaturised, the Doctor and Leela found themselves spinning round and round in a rushing crimson whirlpool, as the Doctor's bloodstream carried them along the spinal cord, towards the menace that lurked in his brain ...

7
Mind Hunt

Like swimmers carried to the bank of a rushing river, the crimson tide deposited the cloned Doctor and Leela on to a solid, lumpy, blue and pink surface, in a gloomy, echoing tunnel. The Doctor helped Leela to her feet. 'We must be somewhere near the top of the spinal column ...' He looked round interestedly. 'Well, what do you think?'

Leela wasn't quite sure what to say. 'I don't know what to think, I've never been inside anybody's head before.' Politely she added, 'It's very interesting.'

'Thank you,' said the Doctor, with equal politeness.

'Why aren't we wet?'

'Because we're too small to break the surface tension ...'

A kind of abbreviated lightning-flash crackled over their heads and zipped away into the distance.

'What was that?'

'Oh, just a passing thought,' said the Doctor airily. 'Electrochemical reaction in the synapses. Leg wants to move, probably ...'

The leg of the tied-down Doctor flailed violently, kicking against the restraining straps. Marius looked worried. 'Don't think he can hold out much longer, the virus seems to be strengthening its grip.'

From the visiphone screen Lowe said angrily, 'Professor Marius! You have not replied to my ultimatum. I can destroy this Centre!'

Marius swung round, holding up his hand. 'No, wait! I agree to your terms. I have no further use for the Doctor, he's yours whenever you want.'

'A wise decision,' said Lowe coldly. 'Tell me, Professor, is the reject Leela with you?'

'No, as you can see, there's simply myself and my assistants. She's somewhere in the Foundation, I've no idea where.'

'No matter. She will be found and destroyed. Stay where you are—we are on our way.' The visiphone went blank.

Marius moved to the doorway and called softly, 'Leela?'

Leela hurried into the room, K9 at her heels.

'They're coming, Leela,' whispered Marius urgently. 'We've got to hold them off for at least ten minutes. Can you do that?'

'Can I borrow K9?'

'Yes, certainly. K9, co-operate with Leela.'

'Master.'

Leela looked down at her ally. 'We'll have to wait for them in the corridor. If we could just make some sort of barrier ...'

'Re-check!' said K9 firmly. 'First we must eliminate the service shaft.'

Leela was pleased to see K9 had good strategic sense. 'Yes, of course, otherwise they can attack us from behind ... What we'll do—'

Marius broke in on their planning session. 'Whatever you're going to do, I should get on with it. We haven't got much time.'

Leela took command. 'K9, you go and destroy the shaft, and then meet me back here.'

'Affirmative.'

They moved off, K9 in one direction, Leela in the other.

'Suppose they fail?' asked Parsons gloomily. He was beginning to feel that their success depended on increasingly strange allies. First two cloned miniatures, now a savage and a robot dog.

Marius crossed to a security locker, opened it and took out two hand-blasters. 'Ever used one of these?'

He pressed one of the weapons into his assistant's hand. 'Here, take it. If by any chance I am taken over by the virus, I hope you won't hesitate to use that blaster on me. Because if you are taken over, I shall certainly use mine on you. Whatever happens, we must give the Doctor his ten minutes.'

'I understand, sir,' said Parsons loyally, hiding the blaster beneath his gown.

The cloned Doctor and Leela were trudging through a sort of soft swampy grotto, festooned with hanging veils of tissue and fine, fungoid webs. Everything was enveloped in murky gloom, though from time to time a bright, lightning-like thought-flash zipped by overhead.

'Doctor,' said Leela reproachfully, 'I do not think you have any idea where we're going.'

'What do you mean, no idea? We're travelling along my neural pathways, looking for a sort of bridge, a crossover point between left and right lobe.'

'Is that where the virus will be?'

'Well, since it seems to be able to control both conscious and unconscious functions, it's a good place to start looking.'

'Suppose we meet it?'

'I don't think we will, not just yet. It came through the optic nerve. We're still somewhere between the spinal cord and the cerebellum. But keep your eyes open for tissue degeneration.'

'Like this?' Leela jabbed her foot at a darker patch of the tissue that surrounded them.

The Doctor winced. 'Steady, that's *me* you're kicking!'

'Sorry,' said Leela penitently. They hurried on.

Behind them, white formless shapes were gathering, trailing them through the neural pathways. The Doctor's body was preparing to deal with the alien intruders...

K9 glided back to Leela. 'Mission accomplished,' he announced proudly. 'Service shaft destroyed—Mistress.'

'Thank you, K9. Now what we need is some sort of barrier.'

K9's blaster-nozzle protruded and he blasted the opposite wall and ceiling with maximum force. Immediately most of the ceiling crashed down. K9 fired again, and a chunk of wall landed on top of it, making a wall of rubble across the corridor.

'Acceptable?' enquired K9.

'Perfect! Thank you, K9.'

'There is no need for gratitude. I am an automaton.'

Leela was scanning the corridor ahead. 'Really?'

'I am without emotional circuits. Only memory and awareness.' All the same, K9's tail antenna was wagging gently. He, too, was scanning the corridor and his sensors picked up the sound of the enemies' approach before they could be seen. 'Attention, hostiles approaching!'

K9 drew back, and Leela took shelter behind a chunk of rubble.

Lowe appeared, with Cruickshank and a number of other Centre staff behind him. All had the metallic rash around the eyes, and all were carrying blasters.

Lowe raised a hand to halt his little army. 'It is the reject.' He moved cautiously forward and peered across the barrier. 'Leela,' he called. 'Leela! Bring me the Doctor!'

'Come and get him,' shouted Leela, and opened fire.

Lowe and his men fired back, and a fierce blaster-battle raged across the barricade.

The Doctor moaned and writhed in his bonds.

Marius checked his wrist chronometer. 'Less than eight minutes to go. Anything, Parsons?'

Parsons was studying Leela's tissue sample under a computerised electron microscope, in the desperate hope of finding some explanation of her immunity from the disease. He studied the computer read-out screen. 'It's all here, sir. Leela's tissue profile, adaptation, disease resistance ...'

'Bit of a mongrel, isn't she,' said Marius thoughtfully. 'Probably explains why her race survived. But no sign of any physical immunity.'

'There's a wide range of possible blood characteristics, sir,' the nurse pointed out. 'It will take hours to check them all.'

'On the other hand it could be a psychological factor,' mused Marius. 'Something in her mind, her way of looking at things.'

There was a crackle of blaster-fire from outside the room, and a yell of triumph from Leela as she scored a hit. 'Aggression?' suggested Parsons.

'Determination, stamina,' said Marius. 'The predator's instinct!'

Leela ducked instinctively as another thought-flash whizzed over her head.

The Doctor looked proudly around him. 'You'd never think it was the most advanced computer system ever, would you?'

Leela pointed to a glowing, knotted mass of tissue hanging just ahead of them. 'Ugh, what's that?'

'That is why my brain is so much superior to yours,' said the Doctor huffily. 'It's a superganglion . . .'

Leela wasn't listening. 'Doctor, I can sense danger,' she whispered.

'Rubbish! If there was any danger about, I'd be the first to sense it. I know this brain like the back of my hand. What do you know about brains anyway?'

'All right, all right, don't get excited,' said Leela. It was a pity the Doctor's bad temper had been cloned along with the rest of him.

'I'll get excited if I like, it's my brain! Do you want

to know something?'

'Not particularly!'

'Well, I'll tell you anyway. Somebody once tried to build a machine as efficient as the brain. Trouble was, it would have had to be bigger than London—you remember London?—and powered by the entire European grid. And that was only a human brain, mine is much more complex. Left and right side working in unison via these specialised neural ganglia, thus combining data storage retrieval with logical inference and the intuitive leap—' The Doctor broke off. 'Are you listening, Leela?'

'Yes,' said Leela, though she'd hardly heard a word.

They'd reached another massive complex of glowing, twisted ganglia. The Doctor pointed, rather like a guide displaying the crown jewels. 'That is the reflex link,' he said impressively. 'With that I can tune myself in to the Time Lord intelligentsia—a thousand superbrains in one!'

'Why don't you do it then?' suggested Leela. She was beginning to get tired of being lectured. As far as she was concerned, they needed all the help they could get.

The Doctor coughed. 'Ah well, as it happens, I lost that particular faculty when they kicked me out ...'

'They kicked you out?' asked Leela, intrigued. She knew little of the Doctor's past history.

The Doctor was studying another tangle of ganglia further down the tunnel. 'Come and look here, Leela, these connections have been severed.' The Doctor studied the rent. 'Hullo ...'

Leela popped her head through the other side of the gap. 'Hullo!'

'Don't be funny,' said the Doctor disapprovingly.

'Doctor, you're wasting time, we've got to keep moving in.'

'No, don't you see, this is recent damage, Leela.'

'The virus?'

'What else? We must be getting close!'

A white blob dropped from nowhere to land on Leela's shoulders. She screamed and tried to throw it off, but another followed, and then another, until she was covered in the billowing globular shapes. 'Doctor, help me,' she screamed.

'I can't! It's my body's defence mechanisms, my own phagocytes. Use your knife!'

Leela drew her knife and slashed desperately about her, but the number of attacking phagocytes seemed limitless, and soon she disappeared from view buried beneath the seething white forms.

With sudden inspiration, the Doctor dashed to the opposite side of the tunnel, grabbed two dangling nerve-ends and thrust them together. There was a crackle and a flash, and suddenly the army of phagocytes began moving away from Leela, disappearing down the tunnel as if summoned by some distant alarm.

The Doctor helped her to her feet.

'What did you do?'

'Gave them a faked alarm call. I think I told them my liver was disintegrating!'

'That's very clever, Doctor!'

'I know it's very clever,' agreed the Doctor. 'Come on!'

*

In the isolation ward the Doctor struggled to reach the small of his back. His whole body arched and he gave a groan.

'What's happening?'

Marius shrugged. 'No idea. But it proves they're in there ... some sensitive area ...'

They heard more blaster-fire from the corridor outside. It was closer now, as though K9 and Leela were being driven back.

Marius looked at the chronometer. 'Seven and a half minutes to go.' He sighed. 'Not much chance of success now ...'

Lowe's attacking army seemed to be unlimited. Between them Leela and K9 had shot a good many down, but there were always others who stepped forward to take their place. Lowe and his aides seemed to have managed to infect most of the staff of the Centre between them.

Cruickshank, more infected and more fanatical than the rest, hurtled over the barrier in a desperate leap— and K9 shot him down. Cruickshank fell dying directly in front of K9—and a sudden lightning-flash crackled between his eyes and K9's eye-screen.

In a slurred, dragging voice K9 said, 'Contact has been made—Master ...'

From the other side of the barrier Lowe screamed, 'Kill her, K9! Kill the reject!'

'Affirmative. Kill the reject,' droned K9 obediently. He swung round. Leela was moving about further along the barricade, ducking from one piece of cover to another, returning the fire of Lowe and his men.

Vastly outnumbered, she was enjoying herself enormously.

Absorbed in her battle, she didn't notice K9 gliding towards her, the nozzle of his blaster aimed at her back . . .

8

Interface

The Doctor paused at a gaping, blackened split in the tunnel wall. 'After you, Leela.'

'Are you afraid?'

'Not necessarily,' said the Doctor a little defensively. 'But from now on we're right on the trail of the virus. That's the path it took.'

'Where to?'

'Well if I knew that I wouldn't have brought you along. This is where your tracking skills come in.'

Leela nodded and drew her knife. She slipped through the dark, sinister-looking gap, the Doctor close behind her.

Not for the first time, Leela's uncanny instinct saved her life. Sensing danger she swung round—to find K9's blaster covering her. K9 fired, but she was already hurling herself through the air in a flying leap. K9's blaster-bolt missed, and Leela landed awkwardly. She twisted her foot on a chunk of rubble, and pitched forward. Her head thumped against the wall.

K9 wheeled to face Lowe who was clambering over the barricade. In a slurred voice K9 said, 'Reject liquidated. K9 into self-regeneration—non-functional ...' K9's eye-screen went dim, and all his antennae drooped. He glided slowly over to the wall beside Leela, bumped his nose against it and stayed motionless.

Lowe dropped down over the barricade, saw the knocked-out Leela and drew the obvious conclusion. The reject was dead, the automaton de-activated. He had no further interest in either of them. 'Good—and now for the Doctor,' he whispered exultantly. He headed for the door of the isolation ward.

Leela said, 'Ouch!' and clutched the back of her head.

'What is it, Leela? What's the matter?'

'Something banged my head . . . a real thud . . .'

'Not in here, Leela, that must have been your outside head.'

'Oh, well, that's all right then.'

'No it isn't,' said the Doctor seriously. 'You and I have only got a limited life in here as it is. Your outside self and your inside self are made of the same tissue. If your outside self is hurt, then you feel the shock. And if your outside self is killed . . .'

Leela shuddered. 'We'd better make the most of the next six minutes then.'

They moved on their way, following the blackened trail of virus damage. It was very plain now, and it led them at last to what looked like a colossal chasm. Into the chasm projected a kind of bridge, a narrow strip of tissue arching up into the darkness. But the bridge stopped, abruptly, half-way across. It was a bridge to nowhere. A rushing wind filled the air, howling through the depths of the chasm.

'Where are we?' whispered Leela.

'This is the gap between one side of my mind and

the other.'

'But it's dark on the other side!'

'Well of course it's dark, Leela. It's the gap between logic and imagination. You can't *see* one side from the other side.'

'But it is there? There is something on the other side?'

'This is the mind-brain interface, Leela—at least, I think it is.' The Doctor gestured expansively. 'There's the mind and there's the brain. Two things entirely different, yet part of the same thing.'

'Like the land and the sea?'

Pleased with her understanding, the Doctor said, 'That's right, Leela. That's exactly right!'

Leela stared down into the chasm. 'It's very deep!'

The Doctor looked thoughtfully into the darkness of his own unconscious mind. 'Yes ... sometimes I don't quite understand it myself!'

Giving Leela one end of his scarf to hold, the Doctor began edging his way across the narrow bridge.

Leela followed nervously. The ridge of tissue was appallingly narrow and it felt spongy and unreliable beneath her feet. The wind howled around her, plucking at her clothes. Several times she came close to losing her balance.

When he got to the point where the bridge appeared to vanish the Doctor stepped confidently off into blackness. He vanished. His scarf vanished too, except for the section Leela was holding. Leela hesitated. There came an indignant tug from the invisible Doctor on the end of the invisible bit of scarf. Leela closed her eyes and stepped off into nothingness ...

*

Marius looked at his chronometer. 'Five minutes to go . . .' he said despondently.

'Don't move, Professor,' said a harsh triumphant voice. Lowe was covering him from the doorway.

Parsons made a desperate attempt to reach the blaster under his gown. Lowe swung his blaster and shot him down. He turned the blaster back on Marius. 'Release the Doctor.'

'No,' said Marius defiantly. 'No, I can't!'

Lowe came menacingly forward. When he stood face to face with Marius, a jagged lightning-streak flashed between his own forehead and the professor's.

'Release him,' said Lowe again.

In a slurred, dragging voice Marius said, 'Contact has been made.' He moved to unfasten the straps.

(Unseen, Marius's nurse crouched down behind the cloning booth, too terrified to move.)

'We must make contact with the Nucleus,' said Lowe eagerly.

With the virus in control of his mind, all Marius's loyalties were now devoted to the Purpose. 'No, wait,' he said. 'The Nucleus is in danger.'

'What?' snarled Lowe.

Marius's words seemed to come tumbling out. 'Micro-cloned copies have been injected into the brain to hunt down and destroy the Nucleus . . . If they succeed . . .'

'They must not succeed!'

'We can't stop them,' babbled Marius. 'There is no time.'

'I say we must!' roared Lowe. 'We must!'

(Unseen, the nurse began edging towards the door.)

*

Outside in the corridor, K9 came slowly back to life. Leela, too, was beginning to revive. K9 glided up to her and sent out a probe from his head to touch her forehead. 'Mistress!' he called.

A mild electric tingle brought Leela to full consciousness, and she scrambled to her feet. 'Why did you attack me?'

'I had to. I was temporarily overpowered, and my motivational circuits were in confusion. I have now fully regenerated, and await your further orders—Mistress.'

'Where are our enemies? Have they captured the Doctor?'

Sadly K9 said, 'Affirmative, Mistress.'

Suddenly the nurse slipped out of the isolation ward and ran down the corridor towards them. 'They've got Professor Marius—he's been taken over by the virus. They've killed Doctor Parsons ...'

She began to sob. Leela grabbed her by the shoulders and shook her hard. 'What are they doing now?'

'They're cloning Lowe. Marius is going to inject him into the Doctor's brain.'

Leela headed for the ward door. 'We'd better stop them.'

K9 glided forward to bar her way. 'Negative!'

'Why?'

'We cannot interfere while there is still a possibility that the micro-clone of the Doctor will succeed in destroying the Nucleus. We must wait.'

The micro-cloned Leela found herself following the Doctor across the other side of the narrow bridge. The only difference was that now instead of not seeing where she was going, she couldn't see where she'd been. The brain storm howled round them with renewed force now, and she wondered when the other side of the chasm would come in sight.

'Bracing, isn't it?' shouted the Doctor.

'Very!' said Leela grimly.

The Doctor looked around him. They were facing a great cliff of sheer, solid blackness. There was blackness above and below them, blackness on every side. 'Magnificent, isn't it? The interface! The mind, unsullied by a single thought!'

'Where are we going?' asked Leela practically.

'Into the land of dreams and fantasy, Leela ...'

Professor Marius bent over the deformed body of the Doctor, a hypodermic in his hand. The colourless fluid inside it held the micro-cloned body of Lowe. Carefully Marius injected the fluid into the Doctor's head ...

A horrible gurgling voice came from the Doctor's twisted mouth. 'Hurry, hurry. They are closing in. Hurry, hurry, hurry ...'

With the panic-stricken voice of the Nucleus urging him on, Lowe raced through the Doctor's brain. He forced his way through the blackened split in the neural tissue, and raced recklessly across the narrow windswept bridge ...

The Doctor and Leela meanwhile were forcing their way through a tunnel in what looked and felt like

black, shiny rock. 'Is this your land of dreams? 'asked
Leela.

'Well, on the way to it ...'

They emerged from the cleft into an enormous
cavern, bigger than a thousand cathedrals. Huge silver
pillars stretched away into the immeasurable distance.

Near-by, on the floor of the cavern, was a twisted
honeycomb of rock, a strange distorted growth that
was obviously out of place.

'There it is,' said the Doctor quietly. They began
hurrying towards it. As they came closer, Leela could
see that something living was stirring inside the rock.
She caught a glimpse of lashing tentacles, the evil
gleam of a bulbous eye.

'The evil thing,' breathed Leela. She paused to
listen. 'And another follows, close behind us, Doctor.
We're trapped!'

9
Nucleus

Before the Doctor could speak, Leela drew her blaster and ran back towards the tunnel.

The Doctor walked forward to confront his enemy. As he got closer to the twisted honeycomb, he saw through the many holes and gaps that some strange living creature seemed to permeate the whole structure. He saw waving antennae, glistening wet red flesh, and a bulbous black eye that seemed to swivel to and fro in search of him. From the little he could see, thought the Doctor, it was probably just as well that the rest was concealed.

He strode up to the rock and said, 'Hullo! Who are you?'

A slobbering, gurgling voice said arrogantly, 'I am the Nucleus!'

'You're trespassing, you know,' said the Doctor reprovingly. 'Disturbing my unconscious, affecting my metabolism——' He paused. 'Nucleus of what?'

'The Nucleus of the Swarm,' gurgled the voice.

'I see,' said the Doctor thoughtfully. Then he snapped, 'Why did you choose my brain?'

'Because of your intelligence.'

'Well, I can understand that,' said the Doctor. 'But you've no right——'

'I have every right,' interrupted the hateful voice. 'It is the right of every creature across the Universe to survive, multiply and perpetuate its species ... How else does the predator exist? And we are all predators, Doctor. We kill, we devour to live. Survival is all! You agree?'

'Oh yes, I do. And on your own argument, I have a perfect right to dispose of you.'

'Of course! The law is survival of the fittest!'

A long whip-like tentacle lashed out at the Doctor's face, nicking his cheek. The Doctor touched the cut, and looked at the little smear of blood on his fingers. 'Touché!' he said wryly.

'Your time is running short,' sneered the Nucleus. 'How do you intend to dispose of me? You have no weapons and in minutes you will cease to exist!'

The Doctor said nothing. The Nucleus began a long, ranting speech of self-justification. 'I am the Virus and the Nucleus of the Swarm. For millennia we have hung dormant in space, waiting for the right carrier to come along ...'

This was too much for the Doctor. 'Carrier?' he said indignantly. 'What do you mean, carrier? I'm not a porter!'

The Nucleus ignored him. 'Consider the human species. They send hordes of settlers across the galaxy to breed, multiply, conquer and dominate. We have as much right to conquer them, as they have to strike out across the stars.'

'But you intend to dominate both worlds,' said the Doctor sombrely. 'The micro- and the macro-cosm.'

'We have waited, waited,' said the gloating voice.

'Waited in the cold wastes of space for mankind to come. Now we have not only space but time itself within our grasp!'

'Time?'

'Through you—*Time Lord*!'

So, thought the Doctor grimly, the Nucleus knew. Now more than ever it had to be destroyed . . .

Leela waited in the long black tunnel, knife in hand. She could almost sense the approach of her enemy.

A figure lurched into view and she sprang—then jumped back in horror. A mass of pulsing white phagocytes was covering Lowe's body. Only his incredible fanaticism could have enabled him to keep moving.

Leela hesitated, knife poised, looking for the human target under the pulsating mass. Somehow Lowe managed to fire, and a blaster-bolt seared Leela's side. She staggered back, drew her own blaster, and fired again and again. Lowe's body slumped down, and the phagocytes swarmed over it, devouring it. Leela ran back along the tunnel.

'So, Doctor,' concluded the Nucleus triumphantly, 'How can you puny creatures compare yourselves to us, the Swarm? The new masters of time, space and the cosmos!'

'New masters?' said the Doctor grimly. 'Not if I can help it!'

'But you cannot! Your time is up. You have fallen for my stratagem. Already you cease to exist!'

The Doctor touched a hand to his face. It felt insubstantial, paper-thin ... He could feel cracks appearing. Too late the Doctor remembered that he was only a carbon copy with a strictly limited life—a life that looked like ending before its work was done ...

Leela came staggering back into the great cave, blaster in hand, and the Doctor shouted, 'Leela, the blaster! Give it to me!'

She threw it, the Doctor caught it and swung round to fire at the rock. Already the black rock was splitting as the Nucleus struggled to escape ... Eyes dimming, hand shaking, the Doctor fired at the rock, muttering, 'Get out of my brain! Get out of my brain ...' The blaster dropped from his hand. He staggered and fell.

Leela ran to kneel beside him. Her body was dry and cracking too, and she could feel herself fading away. 'Has it gone, Doctor?'

The Doctor pointed. The honeycomb rock was smashed to pieces, and the fragments were rapidly crumbling to black dust. Of the Nucleus there was no sign.

The Doctor struggled to rise. 'The tear duct,' he muttered. 'Must get to the tear duct ...'

Leela tried to help him, but he faded away in her arms, leaving only a bundle of clothes and a long scarf. Then these too vanished.

Next, Leela herself vanished. For a moment a knife and a lock of long hair lay on the cavern floor, then faded and vanished. The real Doctor and Leela, the originals, were still alive and struggling in the Foundation, but their carbon copies were no more.

Something red and glistening scuttled away through

the caverns of the Doctor's mind ... towards the tear duct.

The Doctor's face was almost entirely covered with the metallic rash by now. A tear welled from the corner of one eye. Marius, his own face affected by the rapidly spreading virus, caught the tear on a glass rod and transferred it to a glass dish.

Lowe, the real Lowe, glared malevolently at the tiny drop of fluid. 'Destroy them. Destroy them now!'

Marius shook his head. 'No. We must find out what happened in there. We must restore them to their full size and interrogate them while there is still time ...'

He carried the dish over to the cloning booth, reversed the RDS controls as the Doctor had shown him, switched on the machine, closed the booth door and stepped back.

There was a hum of power, and a shape began to form inside the booth. But it was not the shape of the Doctor or Leela ... It was not a humanoid shape at all ...

At the same time the signs of the virus infection were receding from the Doctor's face with incredible speed. Soon he was completely himself again. His eyes opened and he looked round alertly.

Lowe opened the door, and stepped back reverently. A horrible, incredible shape was filling the booth. It was blood-red in colour and was as big as a man with a bony glistening body and lashing tentacles. The huge black bulbous eyes swivelled malevolently around the ward. The Doctor's RDS had magnified the Nucleus to full human size.

'Help me,' gurgled the creature. 'Help me out.'

Lowe and one of his infected aides went to help.

'Marius!' hissed the Doctor.

Marius swung round, and the Doctor saw the virus-rash overspreading his face. 'Oh, no,' he groaned.

'Yes, Doctor,' said Marius complacently. 'Contact has been made. Now I serve the Purpose!'

The Doctor looked at the pulsating creature being lifted from the booth. 'What? And that pathetic crustacean is your leader?'

'You are speaking of the Nucleus, the Nucleus of the Swarm,' snarled Marius.

'Take me to him,' ordered the Nucleus.

Lowe and an aide lifted the horrible creature and carried it across to where the Doctor lay on his couch. The Doctor studied the Nucleus thoughtfully. It didn't look as if it could move or even stand unassisted. Perhaps it hadn't grown fully used to its new size. No doubt in time it would adapt, grow strong ... 'Finding the macro-world difficult?' enquired the Doctor affably.

'Soon it will suit me well,' promised the Nucleus.

'I thought I'd got rid of you!'

'You were mistaken. I made use of your escape route, through the eye.'

'Yes, you'd have known about that,' said the Doctor thoughtfully. 'Snooping about in my mind ...'

'Another mistake, Time Lord—and a costly one for you. Now, thanks to your dimensional stabiliser, I am no longer forced to remain in the micro-world to breed and multiply. My Swarm, when it is hatched on Titan, will no longer take the form of invisible microbes, weak and prey to all, but mighty and invulnerable creatures. Invincible! The Age of Man is over, Doctor. The Age of the Virus has begun!'

'I've heard all that before,' said the Doctor scornfully. 'You megalomaniacs are all the same!'

Angry at the Doctor's blasphemy, Marius leaned over him, staring hard into his eyes. A lightning-tentacle flashed between his eyes and the Doctor's—and rebounded on to Marius again. He staggered back.

The Doctor felt a sudden surge of hope. He was immune! Perhaps because he'd survived such a massive attack, perhaps for some other reason, the virus could no longer take over his mind. Now he could really fight back.

His relief was short-lived. Lowe stepped forward, face twisted with anger, raising his blaster.

'No, not yet,' commanded the Nucleus.

Apparently, it felt that a quick death was too good for the Doctor. 'We shall take him with us to Titan—to be consumed by the Swarm!'

10

The Antidote

Leela looked admiringly at herself in the mirror set into the locker door. She'd broken open a first-aid locker in the reception area, and was using a random assortment of ointments and dressings to produce a fair approximation of someone in the first stages of virus infection. A nurse's robe she found hanging in another locker completed her disguise. 'How do I look, K9?'

'Friend, Mistress,' said K9, failing to understand her question.

Leela checked the blaster hidden under her robe. 'If I can just get close enough to that Nucleus, it'll see how friendly I am.'

'Hostiles approaching, Mistress,' warned K9. 'With the Doctor.'

They ducked into a doorway for cover.

An extraordinary procession was coming down the main corridor. First came the heaving, pulsating Nucleus, its breath gurgling liquidly in its throat. Lowe and a medic were supporting it between them. Behind them came the Doctor, firmly strapped down to a hospital trolley, pushed by Marius.

The Nucleus was growing impatient. 'Hurry! Hurry! It is time for the spawning. I must go to the place prepared on Titan.'

From the corner of his eye Marius caught sight of Leela's uniform. 'Nurse, take over here. I must assist with the Nucleus!'

Hesitantly Leela came forward. Marius showed no signs of recognising her, perhaps because of her disguise, perhaps because personality meant little to those who served the Purpose. Marius let Leela take over the pushing of the trolley, while he went to help Lowe and the others with the cumbersome, constantly complaining Nucleus.

The Doctor looked up. 'Your eye make-up's running, Leela!' he whispered.

'Ssh!' reproved Leela. She slipped the knife from under her coat and began sawing at the Doctor's bonds.

By the time they reached the TARDIS, standing forgotten in its corner, the Doctor was free.

With a sudden shove, Leela whizzed the trolley towards the TARDIS door.

Marius turned. 'Nurse, not that way!'

But it was too late. The Doctor sprang from the trolley, opened the TARDIS door and leaped inside. K9, who had been lurking behind the TARDIS, whizzed round to the front and followed the Doctor in. Hampered by the cumbersome Nucleus, it took Lowe and Marius too long to react. Lowe detached himself from the group and raised his blaster. Leela fired a quick blast at random. It missed, but it was enough to spoil Lowe's aim. The blaster-bolt sizzled harmlessly over her head, and seconds later she was safe inside the TARDIS with the others. The door closed behind her.

'They have escaped,' screamed Lowe.

'They are trapped,' corrected the Nucleus. 'Without its missing component, the Doctor's craft cannot move. Marius, you will stay here, to make sure the Doctor does not escape. Recruit other host bodies. When the Doctor emerges, recapture him, and join us on Titan.'

Marius bowed his head in assent.

Lowe and the others carried the Nucleus towards the airlock. A Foundation shuttle craft stood fuelled and ready in the departure bay. Soon the Nucleus would be on Titan, and the spawning could begin.

Thankfully Leela peeled off the last of her disguise. 'Well, Doctor, now what?'

'Now nothing,' said the Doctor gloomily. He was watching the airlock door on the scanner, as it closed behind the Nucleus and its attendants.

'Doctor, if we can get to Titan first we can still beat that horrible thing.'

'Well, we can't. The dimensional stabiliser's still in the isolation ward. Without it the TARDIS won't move an inch.'

'So there's nothing we can do?' asked Leela disgustedly.

'Did I say that, K9?' The Doctor looked down. K9 was gliding inquisitively round the TARDIS control room, pausing to sniff, or rather to sense, various interesting pieces of equipment. 'Listen to me, K9! Do you think you could go out there and poleaxe Marius?'

K9 said 'Query: please clarify term "poleaxe".'

'Knock him out!'

'Affirmative. My weaponry has four levels of intensity. Kill, stun, paralyse ...

'No, no, no, not kill. Just knock him out, eh?'

'Affirmative.'

'Good dog!'

The Doctor looked at the scanner screen. After hovering indecisively for some time, Marius was heading for the reception desk.

'Off you go then, K9.' He opened the TARDIS door and K9 glided out.

Marius was at the reception desk microphone. 'All senior staff to reception. This is Professor Marius. Senior staff to reception ...' He looked down coldly as K9 approached. With the virus now controlling his mind, Marius could no longer understand the streak of sentiment that had caused him to want a computer in the shape of a dog. 'K9,' he said coldly, 'I no longer need you.'

K9 blasted him, and Marius slumped to the ground. The Doctor and Leela rushed from the TARDIS, picked up Marius, threw him on to the trolley that had been used for the Doctor, and whizzed him away.

The trolley sped along the corridors and shot into the isolation ward. The Doctor burst into a flurry of activity. He took a blood sample from his own finger, mounted it on a slide, then turned to Leela. 'Your turn, Leela, finger! Quickly, we haven't got a moment to spare.'

Leela winced as the Doctor pricked her finger with the little scalpel.

The Doctor smiled. 'Come on, Leela, not frightened of a spot of blood are you—mighty hunter!'

'Just hurry up,' said Leela, sucking her finger.

The Doctor mounted Leela's blood sample next to his own and slid the slide into the computerised electron microscope. Leela watched him, baffled. 'Haven't we been through all this before?'

'I had the virus then—I'm immune now. Something must have happened while you and I were inside my head. I want to find out what!' The Doctor switched on the microscope's read-out screen and studied it absorbedly. 'Ah, now that's very interesting.'

Leela looked at the swarming patterns on the screen, her blood sample and the Doctor's side by side. To Leela they looked completely different—but not to the Doctor.

He leaned forward and tapped the screen. 'See that fish-hook shape wriggling about? That's an antibody, the only one you and I have in common. I didn't have that before, so it must be the immunity factor.'

'How did what I have get into your blood?'

'Quite simple. Your clone, which was produced from your tissue, was absorbed into my bloodstream and passed on the immunity to me. All we've got to do is isolate it, analyse it, duplicate it, and inject it into Marius here, and he in turn will be able to cure all the others.'

Leela couldn't believe things were quite that simple. 'What about the Nucleus? What about Titan?'

'One thing at a time, Leela,' said the Doctor reproachfully. 'One thing at a time!'

The Foundation shuttle, sides marked with the red cross, was carrying its strange passengers towards Titan. Lowe was at the controls, while the Nucleus was pulsating on an acceleration couch, surrounded and supported by its taken-over aides. 'Faster, faster!' roared the Nucleus. It was in a slavering frenzy of impatience.

'We can't,' said Lowe. 'Any faster and the motors will burn out.'

'Let them burn out. Once we reach Titan and the breeding tanks, your task is finished.'

'What about the Doctor?'

'He will follow us to Titan, a prisoner. Marius will make sure of that. Faster, now. Use all the fuel! Faster!'

Obediently Lowe thrust the speed-control lever to maximum. The shuttle surged forward with a roar that shook the little cabin.

The Doctor and Leela hovered anxiously over Professor Marius. He had been injected with the antidote some time ago. Now they were waiting to see the results.

'It's working,' whispered Leela. 'Look, Doctor!'

With incredible speed the virus rash was receding from Marius's face. Soon it was completely back to normal.

'Sometimes my brilliance astonishes even me,' murmured the Doctor modestly. 'Come on, Marius, wake up, wake up!'

Marius opened his eyes and peered blearily at them. 'What happened?' He sat up and looked round. 'Where's Parsons?'

'Dead, I'm afraid. Do you remember anything?'

Marius frowned. 'I remember Lowe coming in . . .

94

then there was a flash ... then nothing ... Doctor, did the experiment work?'

'Yes—and no,' said the Doctor ruefully. 'Unfortunately, the Nucleus got away, and the dimensional stabiliser increased it to human size. It's on its way to Titan to breed.'

'And was I taken over?' Marius rubbed a hand over his face, relieved to find it normal.

'Yes, it got you, for a while, Professor. But we've found the immunity factor. So we're safe here, at least for the time being ...'

Marius was overjoyed. 'The immunity factor? What was it?'

'It was something in Leela, something we all missed.' He handed Marius a phial of milky liquid. 'This is the antidote, but you'll have to make a great deal more. And Professor, if those antibodies can confer immunity, they can be developed to attack the Nucleus!'

'Attack the Nucleus?' said Marius, alarmed. 'That will be highly dangerous, Doctor.'

'Of course it's dangerous! But if we allow the Nucleus to breed and swarm, it will go through the entire galaxy like a plague of giant locusts.'

'But even if we develop a way to destroy the virus, will you be able to get it to Titan on time?'

'Yes!' said the Doctor triumphantly. He crossed to the booth and picked up the complex electronic equipment. 'Now I've got this back, we can use the TARDIS...'

The huge bubbling tank was completely walled-in,

the only entrance by a heavy metal door.

Safran looked through the thick plasti-glass viewing window set into the door. The giant tank was filled with a bubbling, seething fluid. He studied a control panel beside the door. Temperature, nutrients, atmosphere, all were exactly right.

With a smile of pride, Safran crossed to a space-radio set up in the corner and leaned over the speaker-microphone. 'Safran on Titan. Safran on Titan. The Hive is prepared. The breeding tanks are ready. Temperature and humidity are set.'

Safran glanced back proudly at the seething, glowing tank. 'I await your arrival—and the generation of the Swarm!'

The entire control cabin was shuddering with the speed of the shuttle's flight. But still the Nucleus was not satisfied. 'Faster, faster!' it screamed.

'There is no more I can do,' shouted Lowe helplessly. 'We have already reached maximum speed!'

'We must go faster, Lowe,' it roared. 'The time for spawning is very close ...'

The shuttle sped on. As soon as it arrived on Titan, mankind would be doomed ...

11

The Hive

The isolation ward was a scene of bustling activity again. Leela, the Doctor and K9 had been scouring the Foundation for infected medics, knocking them out, and dragging them back to the isolation ward where they were forcibly injected with the antidote. When a sufficient number of medics had been cured, they were set to work manufacturing supplies of the antidote and sent out in teams to cure their fellow workers. It would be a long time before everything was back to normal, but slowly the Foundation was coming back to life.

Leela had quite enjoyed that part of the proceedings, but now she was restless again. The Doctor and Marius were busily trying to produce a killer-virus that would destroy the Nucleus and its Swarm. It seemed to be a very long and complicated business, and Leela soon grew tired of watching masked and robed medics bustling about with dishes of virus-culture.

'How much longer, Doctor?' she asked impatiently.

The Doctor was absorbed in his work. 'Can't rush these things, they're breeding them as fast as they can. K9's linked to the computer-microscope. He'll tell us when we've got the most powerful strain.'

Leela brooded for a while. 'Why don't we just blow

up Titan?' she suggested cheerfully. 'Nucleus, breeding tanks and all!'

The Doctor looked reprovingly at her. 'That's your answer to everything, isn't it? Knock it on the head!'

'Well, it's effective, isn't it? Smash it, once and for all...'

'With what?' demanded the Doctor. 'This happens to be a hospital, not an arsenal!'

'All right,' said Leela sulkily. 'How are you going to fight it?'

K9 bustled forward importantly. 'Confirm strain C531 has optimum lethal capacity.'

Marius hurried up to them, in a state of great excitement. 'Doctor, we've done it! Congratulations!' He turned to his assistants. 'Manufacture a batch of C531 immediately. Hurry now, there isn't a moment to be lost!'

The Doctor leaned down and patted K9 on the head. 'Thank you,' he said solemnly.

Leela was impatient. 'And now what?'

'We just chuck it into the breeding tank, and wait for it to attack the Nucleus the same way the virus attacked us ... microscopically! Neat, don't you think?'

'Oh, is that all?' asked Leela satirically. '*If* we can get to Titan in time, *if* we can get past Lowe and the others, *if* it works when we finally let it into the breeding tank——' She checked herself. 'I thought you didn't like killing?'

'I don't.'

'Then why are you doing all this?' asked Leela, confident she'd caught the Doctor out for once.

'The virus has a perfect right to exist *as* a virus—

but not as a giant swarm threatening the galaxy. Everything has its place. Otherwise the delicate balance of the whole cosmos is destroyed!'

'I still say we should blow it up,' muttered Leela sulkily.

Marius came hurrying forward, holding a vacuum-container. 'Doctor, the batch is complete!'

The Doctor took the container in his hands, and stood looking down at it for a moment. 'Good! Now for the TARDIS!'

The Nucleus emerged from the airlock on Titan Base and moved slowly and painfully along the corridors, assisted by its solicitous helpers.

Safran stood waiting at the door of the giant fuel tank. Proudly he opened the hatch and the Nucleus heaved itself to the brim of the tank. 'Remember,' said the gurgling voice, 'I must be protected while I am in the Hive. The future of the Swarm depends on you!'

Lowe and Safran and the aides bowed their heads in reverence. The Nucleus disappeared into the seething tank of nutrient.

Safran stepped back, and closed the door reverently. The breeding of the Swarm was about to begin.

The Doctor and Leela paused by the open door of the TARDIS to say good-bye to Marius and K9.

'Good luck, Doctor,' said Marius.

'Thank you.' The Doctor turned to enter the TARDIS and then paused. 'Oh Professor?'

'Yes?'

'I don't suppose we could borrow K9, could we?' asked the Doctor hopefully.

'Borrow K9—what for?'

'I've got used to having him around—and he can be very useful.'

'Of course, I understand.' Marius looked down. 'K9! Obey the Doctor.'

'Affirmative,' said K9 happily, and disappeared into the TARDIS.

Marius stepped back, the TARDIS door closed and a few minutes later there was a strange, wheezing, groaning sound. The TARDIS disappeared. Marius blinked in mild surprise, and then hurried away. There was still a great deal to do before the Foundation could be got back to normal.

Lowe moved along the gloomy, winding corridors of Titan Base, followed by his medics. All were armed with blasters, and Lowe posted a guard at each main intersection.

When he was satisfied his defences were complete he returned to the great fuel tank and looked through the viewing window.

The Nucleus lay inert, pulsating gently in a sea of bubbling grey jelly. Surrounding it were thousands upon thousands of eggs, round and white, as big as tennis balls. They lay floating on the seething tank of jelly awaiting the moment when it was time for them to hatch ...

By means of a rather nifty feat of navigation, the

Doctor managed to materialise the TARDIS in Supervisor Lowe's office. The visiphone screen showed the interior of the breeding tank. The Doctor studied the seething mass of eggs. 'The breeding season's already under way!'

Leela stared at the screen in alarm. 'Doctor, what is it?'

'It's the Swarm—and it's starting to hatch. We must hurry!'

The Doctor looked out of the office door, and then stepped back.

'What's the matter?' whispered Leela.

'There's a guard coming. He must have heard the TARDIS ...'

Leela motioned to the Doctor to step back, and waited, drawing her blaster.

'Come in!' shouted the Doctor cheerfully.

The guard stepped through the door, blaster at the ready. Leela fired. The guard staggered back. Incredibly he didn't fall, even though he'd been shot at point-blank range. Slowly, painfully, he raised his blaster to cover Leela. She fired again but there was no effect. It wasn't until K9 glided forward and added his blaster-fire to her own that the guard staggered, and finally fell.

'Thank you, K9,' said Leela. 'Doctor, what went wrong? Why didn't my blaster work?'

The Doctor was kneeling by the fallen guard. The man was in an advanced stage of viral infection, face and hands almost covered by the growth of stiff, metallic hair. 'Their internal cell structure must be changing. They're developing a resistance to radiation——'

'Master, I have a problem,' K9 broke in suddenly.

'Offensive capability seriously diminished, reserves ...
very low.' K9's eye-screen went dim, all his antennae
drooped, and he became very still.

'K9's breaking up, my blaster's finished,' said Leela
worriedly. 'Doctor, what are we going to do?'

'Shall we try using our intelligence?'

'Well, if you think that's a good idea,' said Leela
dubiously.

The Doctor was already disappearing down the corridor. 'Come on,' he shouted. 'And you, K9.'

Leela ran after the Doctor and K9 glided after them.

They hadn't got very far before they came to another
intersection—and another guard. They flattened
themselves back against the wall, and the Doctor
whispered, 'K9, you see that guard?'

'Affirmative.'

'I want you to decoy him.'

K9 glided into view. The astonished guard stared
for a moment and then raised his blaster. K9 zig-
zagged wildly, the blaster-bolts missed, and K9 vanished down the corridor with the guard in pursuit.

The Doctor and Leela moved cautiously on. At the
end of the corridor was a gloomy shadowed cavern
lined with enormous gas storage tanks. In the centre
on the other side was the breeding tank. Lowe and
Safran were standing guard outside.

As the Doctor stood considering his next move, K9
glided up behind them, having lost the guard in the
maze of corridors.

'Mission accomplished.'

'Good dog. Your turn now, Leela. See you back at
the TARDIS.'

'Good luck, Doctor,' whispered Leela. 'You know, I still think we should have done what I said!'

'What was that?'

'Blown it up!' said Leela unrepentantly. She sprinted across the open space.

Safran reacted instantly, raising his blaster and firing after her. But Leela had already disappeared down another corridor, and Safran ran off in pursuit.

Only Lowe was left on guard.

'It's up to us now, K9,' whispered the Doctor. 'This may not be easy.'

'Concern is not necessary. I am an automaton.' Without waiting for the Doctor's command, K9 glided forward to draw Lowe's fire.

Lowe fired and missed. K9 fired back, but his powers were failing now and his aim was poor. Lowe fired again, and K9 spun round in a circle, shot blindly forwards, thudded against the side of the tank, close to the door, and stopped there, motionless.

Lowe raised his blaster to finish him off—then saw the Doctor at the tank, vacuum box in one hand, struggling to open the hatch door.

Lowe fired at once—and a freak shot blasted the vacuum box from the Doctor's hands. It flew open with the impact and the precious serum leaked slowly across the floor.

The Doctor stood quite still, shoulders slumped in defeat.

Lowe came up to him, covering him with his blaster. 'Your futile attempt has failed, as we knew it would. Now you will join the Nucleus.' With his free hand, Lowe reached for the breeding-tank door.

'Well, I'd rather not do that, actually,' said the Doctor mildly.

Lowe raised his blaster. 'You have no choice!' He flung open the hatch door. A fierce, whining, buzzing sound filled the air.

The Doctor peered inside. Many of the eggs had broken open by now, and the creatures inside were stirring, waving transparent wings in a blur of speed . . .

'Oh look, they appear to be hatching!' said the Doctor pleasantly. 'Are congratulations in order?'

'You will join the Swarm,' howled Lowe. 'To be consumed! To become part of our Purpose!' With a wave of his blaster, he motioned the Doctor towards the open hatch.

In order to reach the hatch Lowe had moved past K9, who was now directly behind him, apparently inert. But not quite. K9's eye screen lit up, dimly, and his antennae raised. His blaster-nozzle tilted upwards, and using the last vestige of power in his storage batteries, K9 blasted away at Lowe, firing until his power was exhausted. With a choking scream, Lowe staggered and collapsed, falling dead at the Doctor's feet.

'Well done, K9, well done!' breathed the Doctor. He ran to slam the tank door shut. 'Come on, K9, let's get out of here while there's still time. They'll burst out in a minute . . .'

'I cannot, Doctor. All reserves finished,' whispered K9.

'Come *on*,' said the Doctor. Grabbing K9 by a handy antenna he began towing him.

From inside the breeding tank came the fierce

gurgling voice of the Nucleus. 'Come back, Doctor, come back. We need you!'

The Doctor shuddered, and dragged K9 away.

In a patch of shadow Leela waited, motionless, knife in hand.

Safran came cautiously down the corridor. Leela stayed completely still, let him pass her—and then sprang, bearing him to the ground. Her knife rose and fell. Safran gave a brief choking gurgle and went limp.

Leela wiped her knife on the body and straightened up, just as the Doctor towed K9 round the corner.

'Enjoying yourself?' asked the Doctor.

'What about the Nucleus, Doctor? Did you kill it?'

'No, I lost the antibodies!'

'Never mind, Doctor,' said Leela cheerfully, 'I've found the answer—knife them in the neck!'

'Can you do that to a thousand? A thousand thousand? You haven't seen what's hatching in that tank!'

'What are we going to do?'

'I think I've got an idea. Take K9 back to the TARDIS, he's out of juice!'

'But Doctor . . .'

'Move, Leela!'

Leela shrugged, and began towing K9 away. The Doctor snatched up the fallen Lowe's blaster and began running back towards the breeding tank.

There was just one possible chance—and strangely enough, it had been Leela's idea all along . . .

12

Inferno

The buzzing sound was fiercer, louder now when the Doctor reached the storage area. He paused for a moment, looking round him at the looming rows of tanks. 'This one, I think,' he muttered. He spun a wheel and there was a hiss of escaping gas. The Doctor went to a tank on the other side of the one that held the Swarm. Here, too, he opened a locking valve. The gas hissed out ...

The Doctor ran to the hatch on the central tank, and wedged the blaster into an angle of the iron frame which supported it at the foot. Fumbling in his pocket he produced a little ball of fishing line. He unrolled it, fastened one end to the blaster trigger, the other to the handle of the hatch. A massive thudding came from inside the tank, and the Doctor peered through the little window. The Nucleus, swollen now to enormous size, was lurching towards him through the bodies of the hatching swarm. They looked like huge, malevolent dragonflies—and more and more of them were hatching every second.

'Is that you, Time Lord?' roared the Nucleus.

The Doctor's fingers were busily checking the knots in the twine. 'Well, as far as I know, there's no one else except you and me here, so it must be me!' he babbled nonsensically.

'You are finished, Doctor!'

'Not quite,' yelled the Doctor cheerfully. He tied a final knot and checked that the blaster was securely wedged and pointing in the right direction.

'There is no escape for you now,' gloated the Nucleus. 'You are destined to become part of the Purpose...'

The Doctor stepped back. 'Well,' he said thoughtfully, 'that depends how long it's going to take you to get out of there!'

'Fool!' screamed the Nucleus. 'Do you think a metal barrier can hope to contain the Swarm?'

But the Doctor was already tearing back towards the TARDIS.

Tentacles flailing, bulbous black eyes glaring with maniacal rage, the Nucleus hurled its enormous bulk against the inside of the hatchway door. The heavy metal began to bulge outwards.

Behind the maddened Nucleus, the fierce buzzing of the Swarm rose to a pitch of fury ...

The Doctor shot into Lowe's office to find Leela and K9 waiting by the TARDIS door. Fishing the key from around his neck the Doctor opened the door and vanished inside.

'Wait, Doctor!' yelled Leela, and began heaving K9 over the threshold. No sooner were they inside than the door slammed behind them.

The Doctor was already busy at the controls, the central column began its rise and fall, the TARDIS was in flight.

'Why did you not wait for us?' demanded Leela crossly. 'What's the hurry?'

The Doctor leaned back against the TARDIS console, too out of breath to explain the desperate need for haste. 'You'll see, Leela. You'll see!' He turned on the scanner.

With a final tremendous heave, the Nucleus burst open the hatchway door. The string round the blaster trigger tightened and the blaster fired—straight into the methane storage tank opposite. There was a ferocious roar, and a searing pillar of fire sprang from the tank. As the Nucleus lurched from the tank, the swirling gases around it exploded into flame.

With a last gurgling scream, the Nucleus and all its brood vanished, consumed in the roaring sea of fire . . .

Hovering in space at a safe distance, the Doctor and Leela watched the explosion on the TARDIS scanner screen. It was an incredible sight. First the storage station itself sent out a flowering rose of flame. The flames grew and grew until the entire satellite was ablaze, a roaring ball of fire against the blackness of space.

The Doctor chuckled and rubbed his hands, as if warming them against the blaze.

'Is it gone?' asked Leela, awestruck.

'Yes!' said the Doctor exultantly.

'All of it?'

'Yes! Methane atmosphere, you see. Mix well with oxygen, fire off a blaster and run!'

The Doctor leaned down to the recovering K9. 'That was a good idea of mine to blow it up, eh, K9?'

'Affirmative,' said K9 faintly.

'What do you mean, a good idea of yours?' said Leela indignantly. 'That was my idea!'

'What was?'

'To blow it up!'

'Well, then you should be feeling very happy,' said the Doctor, quite unabashed.

'Yes, I am ...' said Leela, smiling. Then her face became serious. 'I suppose we'd better return K9 to Professor Marius. I mean, he isn't ours—is he?'

Things were almost back to normal in the reception area at the Foundation. The icily efficient receptionist sat enthroned behind her desk, ready to book in new arrivals. Lofty consultants strode through the white corridors in solitary majesty, while little groups of nurses and students hurried by. And the Doctor and Leela stood by the open door of the TARDIS, about to say good-bye to Professor Marius and the faithful K9—who was now restored to full vigour, his storage cells recharged.

Everyone was a little sad at the parting. Marius shook the Doctor warmly by the hand. 'Good-bye, Doctor. And thank you for everything you've done for us!'

'It was a pleasure, Professor. And we mustn't forget K9. Do you know, without K9's help, I think we'd all be part of the Swarm by now ...'

Leela nodded. 'We'd never have managed without him—her—it! Sorry, K9.'

'Apologies are not necessary.' Leela bent down and patted him, and K9 said, 'Thank you—Mistress.'

Marius laughed. 'K9 seems to have taken to you.'

Leela nodded without saying anything.

Marius looked from her to the Doctor and came to a decision. He cleared his throat. 'Harrum, well, actually . . .'

'What is it, Professor?'

'Well, actually I have to return to Earth shortly, and you could do me a great favour. Do you think you could possibly——'

Excitedly Leela finished his sentence. 'Take K9 with us?'

'Yes!' beamed Marius.

Leela was ecstatic. 'Please, Doctor, please, please, let's take him!'

Leela looked beseechingly at the Doctor. Before he could say yes or no, K9 shot through the open door of the TARDIS like a dog returning to his kennel.

Marius smiled. 'I'm afraid K9 seems to have made up his own mind.'

Leela dashed into the TARDIS after K9, the Doctor waved good-bye and followed her and the TARDIS door closed. There was a wheezing, groaning sound, and it faded away.

A little sadly, Marius watched it go. Then he brightened. 'Oh, well, I only hope K9 is TARDIS trained!' Chuckling at his own little joke, Professor Marius went on his way. It was nice to think that his old friend was in such good hands . . .